THE
KINGMAKER

DANIEL MARTIN ELLIOTT

Black Rose Writing | Texas

The final approval for this literary material is granted by the author.

First printing

This is a work of fiction. Names, characters, businesses, places, events and incidents are either the products of the author's imagination or used in a fictitious manner. Any resemblance to actual persons, living or dead, or actual events is purely coincidental.

ISBN: 978-1-68433-064-5
PUBLISHED BY BLACK ROSE WRITING
www.blackrosewriting.com

Printed in the United States of America
Suggested Retail Price (SRP) $

The Kingmaker is printed in Traditional Arabic

To my parents, Mark and Nina.

THE
KINGMAKER

PROLOGUE

Peeking through the curtains, he couldn't see where the crowd ended. He dabbed his perspiring forehead with a yellow pocket handkerchief, folded it neatly, and put it on the side table. The heat was unbearable and the rainy season wasn't living up to its name that year. Glancing at his pocket watch, he saw he had about five minutes. He thought of his dad, placing that watch into his little palm on that hot, summer day. He never saw him again. The heat and the watch always reminded him of his father.

Do they extend all the way to the park? That would be something.

A nervous murmur buzzed through the room behind him. Twelve people huddled in small groups, engaged in quiet but intense conversations. They were his inner circle—all friends, mostly family. He smiled as he looked around without focusing on anyone, just content to have them in his life.

He parted the curtains again to look at the crowd, feeling their growing anticipation, waiting for him to appear.

"*Suerte, Papi!*" His daughter said, running up to hug his leg. He couldn't help smiling. Patting her head, he bent down to kiss her forehead and look into her eyes.

"*Mi Cecilia.* After this, let's go for ice cream, eh? What do you think?"

"Yay!"

He kissed her forehead again and stood. His wife, as gorgeous as the day they first met, smiled at him with love in her eyes. He almost missed her that day eight years earlier and would have, had he not forgotten his hat in the café.

"Is this yours?" she asked.

"*Sí.*"

"How do I look?" he asked his wife.

"Like our next president."

He liked the sound of that. He kissed her forehead and looked deep into her eyes, squinting slightly. She squinted back. He didn't have to say the words. Neither did she.

He turned and stepped through the veranda doors.

Chapter One

Man, I hate the goddamn Frankfurt airport. There are times when you get off the plane and have to take a bus to the main terminal, and you roll right past your next flight gate. A48. Yep, there it is. Goddamn stupid bus. And throughout the airport, the staff ride bicycles. Bicycles?! I mean really, Frankfurt airport staff person, do you have to ride a bike in the terminal? What exactly is it that you do?

"Good morning, Margaret!"

"Good morning, Mr. Davis."

Walking through the glass doors of Verge Consulting, Miles Davis entered his kingdom. His step imbued with confidence and purpose, he grabbed the newspapers from the front desk and walked to his corner office. Margaret, a sassy septuagenarian, anticipated his usual arrival time with his mail and phone messages. This morning, however, Miles had arrived a few minutes early, which forced her to hastily grab the bundle and hustle as best she could around her desk. She knew he would not wait for her, and she silently thanked him for that.

"What you got for me?" he asked.

"Well, Henry called and said the Thai prime minister is interested in our proposal."

Good. I really want that one, he thought. "Great. Next?"

"He also said the Nigerians were happy with the meeting

9

last week, and they want to talk again. Lisa has a follow-up with them tomorrow."

The Nigerians, eh? I'm not sure about those guys.

"Good morning, Boss," someone called.

"Morning, Sarah. Next?"

"The BBC wants to interview you."

"About what?"

"Serbia."

"No. I'm not talking about that." *Why does the BBC care about Serbia? Ah, that's right. The new anchorman on the weekend show has a hard on for the Balkans. I think he's dating a model from there. Goddamn Serbia. I hate the Balkans.*

"OK. I'll tell Henry to let them know you aren't available for comment. He also mentioned it looks like Hungary's a go."

Excellent! That would be a difficult, but lucrative, victory.

"Great. Is it confirmed?"

"Not yet."

"Well, shit. If it's happening, we have to be on a flight today!"

"Henry's aware of that."

"Don't I have a meeting with Bill today?"

"Yes."

"What time?"

"Two."

"Hey, Boss," someone called. "Did you hear about Hungary?"

"Hey, Jason. Margaret just told me. Come to my office, and let's chat. I want David and Lisa in on that, too." Miles turned the corner at the end of the hall and headed toward his office.

"Roger that, Boss," Jason said.

"Goddamn it. Bill talks forever. Margaret, please make sure to ring my phone at two-twenty, so I can get the hell out of there."

"Already planned on it."

"Great. Anything else?"

"Yes, sir. A Lauren called. She didn't leave a message, just asked if you were in."

"Lauren?" He stopped and turned toward her, his heart beating a little faster. "French accent?"

"Yes."

"What did she say?"

"Just asked if you were in the office. I said you hadn't arrived yet and asked if she wanted to leave a message. She said to tell you Lauren called. Who is she?"

"No one."

"OK." She knew better than to ask more questions.

"Anything else, Margaret?"

"Just some mail, Mr. Davis. I threw out the junk. Here you go."

"Thanks."

"You're welcome, Mr. Davis."

Miles closed the office door, walked around his mahogany desk, and fell into the plush leather chair. The sun beat through the southeast-facing windows, framing in gold light a picturesque view of the Capitol. The dawn frost had already burned away under the clear, blue sky, yet the remaining moisture still allowed the building to glisten in the morning sun. He noticed the beginnings of scaffolding rising at the base of the dome.

Hmmm. I didn't know they were renovating the Capitol.

He stared at the wall opposite his desk, beyond the small conference table, and reflected on the pictures hanging there. Most were of him in exotic locations or with previous clients, including Shwedagon Pagoda, Clinton, Machu Picchu, Blair, the Parthenon...

I don't have any Africa pictures up there. Maybe something from my trip to Egypt?

Miles Davis was named after the famous jazz musician, but he always joked when people asked him that he preferred John Coltrane. His parents were Chicago Beatniks in the early '50s. "Hippies before being a hippie was cool," his dad used to say. The irony was that his parents didn't listen to jazz. They just liked the name Miles, and their last name was Davis, so it fit.

Could be worse, he thought. *Our last name could have been Gillespie.*

Of normal height and build, Miles had short, scruffy brown hair with a few tinges of gray. Concentrated patches of white congregated at his temples. His blue eyes were framed by thin wire green glasses. He usually had a day-old beard, though he tried to be clean shaven.

Never trust a man who spends more than five minutes on his facial hair. It's either a beard or nothing. Maybe a moustache.

He always wore a suit, either black or light gray, with an open-collared shirt, usually white, and a go-with-anything tie in the breast pocket in case he had to get fancy at the last minute.

Lauren. What the hell does she want?

"Mornin', Boss." David Strasbourg strolled in through the side door. "Thought I heard you come in."

David was six-feet tall with soft, blue eyes and cropped blond hair combed forward. During working hours, that was his clean-cut look, but on weekends, he had the flexibility to spike it up. His suit was light gray and recently dry cleaned, a crisp, tight fold holding down the front of each leg. A striped Gap shirt and solid purple tie lay under his suit jacket. On his feet were pointy Euro shoes and matching purple socks.

David was from Miles' hometown in Illinois. They met two decades earlier, when David was a precocious teen and Miles the campaign manager for a local businessman running for Congress. It was late on a Friday night, and Miles was the last one in the office, poring over the latest poll numbers showing his candidate was down by four points. He fretted over the get-out-the-vote logistics his field coordinator was responsible for and failing miserably at. Frustrated, he cracked open a bottle of cheap whiskey and silently prayed to a god he didn't believe in to throw him a bone. David knocked on the office door a few minutes later.

"What do you know about politics?" Miles asked.

"Nothing, but I want to learn and will do anything."

"I can't pay you."

"That's OK. I'm not doing it for money. I have a paper route in the mornings before school. I can come here every day afterward and on weekends if you need me."

"Why do you want to work in politics?"

"I think it's important, and the right politician can make a difference. Cicero said it's the noblest profession in the world, right?" David smiled.

Miles was immediately reminded of his younger self and liked him instantly. "Something like that." He laughed.

He pointed to a pile of yard signs. "Set those in the ground near the three exit ramps to I-55."

David returned an hour later. "What's next?"

"You have a paper route, right?"

"Yes, since I was nine. I started on my bike. Now I use a car." He glanced proudly at his dark-green 1977 Toyota Camry he bought with his own money. It had over 100,000 miles on it and needed a muffler, but it ran well, and, most importantly, it was his.

"So, you know the town pretty well?"

"Every block like the back of my hand."

By the end of the week, David replaced the field coordinator. Four weeks later, their candidate won the election by three points.

Miles unconsciously furrowed his brow and scrunched up his nose as he opened the *New York Times* to the editorial section. He always read that section first, then started at the front and read the entire paper cover to cover. He did the same thing with the *Washington Post* every day for the last fifteen years.

"Did you hear Henry called?" David asked. "He thinks we've got a meeting with the Thai PM. And it looks like Hungary is a go."

"Yeah, Margaret told me on the way in." Miles replied, half-listening.

"Well, shit! Why aren't you more excited? We've been working on that for months, and it's finally here!"

"Yeah, I know." He set aside the paper and gave a small sigh, trying to shake Lauren from his thoughts. David eyed him curiously.

"OK. I also talked to Henry. He says 'we should get to Budapest as soon as possible. We can have Lisa and John and the rest of the team finish the details today, catch the 5:50 tonight to Frankfurt, get the latest polling and clips on the layover, and be in Budapest by ten tomorrow morning."

"Goddamn Frankfurt. I hate that airport."

"I know, Boss. Me, too, but Munich won't get us there 'til four in the afternoon, and Vienna's full. We could go through Paris but…"

"Good morning, Gentlemen," a sultry voice said through the doorway.

Lisa Goodman was a curvaceous redhead in her late twenties, and this morning she wore a tight, blue dress that accentuated her curves and her dark-red curls. She also wore black tights and smart black pumps. Minimal makeup allowed her natural features to stand out. She had a roundish face with high cheekbones, deep-brown eyes that simultaneously shone with strength and melancholy, and thin red lips that stood in stark contrast to her pale-white skin. She wasn't a beauty in the early 21st century definition of what the glam magazines pandered, but she oozed sex appeal. Manet and Degas would have fought to the death to paint her.

Lisa was a product of elite East-Coast boarding schools and two Ivy League degrees. An only child from divorced parents, she spent countless hours in therapy, which equipped her with enough knowledge and wit to cover her debilitating insecurity and self-esteem issues with a convincing façade. She learned from an early age that focusing on anything outside herself and her family was a viable escape, so she poured herself into whatever she did. Valedictorian in every grade since middle school, she was a three-sport athlete and currently taught yoga part-time. She had also been the lead soprano and actress in most of the school plays. Though she'd had countless boyfriends, none lasted more than a couple weeks. A common refrain among the men she left in her wake was that dating Lisa Goodman was like weathering a hurricane. Most were happy just to get out alive. The latest one, however, seemed to have hit a chord; a two-carat ring dangled on her ring finger.

Along with David and Miles, Lisa rounded out Verge Consulting's A team, the world's preeminent political consulting firm. Over the last couple of years, they helped candidates and political parties at all levels win elections around the world, from San Diego to El Salvador, Stockholm to South Africa,

Jason Stable, one of the rising analysts at the company, trailed behind her with an armful of binders. Deathly skinny with spiky black hair, he wore thick-rimmed glasses, a plaid shirt, a black skinny tie, and tight jeans. David teased him, calling him a reluctant hipster.

"I heard we got Hungary," Lisa said.

"Damn," Dave said. "Word travels fast around here."

I'd go to war with David and Lisa, Miles thought. "Not one hundred percent certain yet, kids. Waiting for Henry to confirm. Let's move on it this morning as if we have to do it."

"Already on it." Lisa took the top binder from Jason's arms

and set it on the conference table before taking a seat behind it. Jason sat beside her. David walked around to sit across from Lisa.

"Here are the latest news clips," Lisa said. "That new intern is awesome. She pulled these together in less than an hour. The only recent public poll is Magyar Hirlap's, and they have the prime minister up six points."

"Of course, they do," David said. "It's a conservative rag that everyone knows is backing Fidesz."

"And their methodology is shit," Lisa added.

"Then why mention them?" David shot back.

"Because it's all there is until we do our own poll, Jackass." She gave him her patented icy stare that had accumulated an impressive body count over the years. David winked and smiled back. Jason looked down, suppressing a smile.

"All right, all right," Miles interrupted. "Enough, you two. I'll read the clips on the plane. Hirlap is shit, but it gives us a starting point. Let's make some decisions. Who do we have on the ground?"

"We can go with Milosz' guy," David said. "Viktor something. We said we'd get in touch with him if we were ever brought into Hungary. He'll know one way or the other that we're working there now, because it's a small country and all. Plus, the other potential partners are either already working with the other side or not playing this time around."

"I think he nailed the last presidential," Lisa said, "within a point or two, if I remember correctly."

"Close," Jason said. "2.2 percent off." He flipped pages to the last election results and how each newspaper and pollster fared. Lisa smiled smugly at her ability to recall that particular fact. David frowned.

"And he goes down to the district level," Lisa added. "I'm sure we could push him down to the settlement level if we wanted to."

Most pollsters who do door-to-door surveys sample at a county or state level because of budgetary constraints, but that increases the potential sampling error.

"Yes," Miles said. "Let's do that. This race is gonna be tight. We gotta get in the weeds here."

"Will do."

"Great. Who do we have for media?"

"James just wrapped up in Argentina and got back last week. I can call to check his availability."

"Text him now. I want him on the flight out with us tonight if he's available."

"On it."

"What's our research strategy?" Miles asked.

"What's our budget?" Lisa countered.

"Let's assume golden."

"OK," David said, running his hand through his hair and massaging the back of his neck. Miles had a similar tick when getting deep into thought that had rubbed off on David over the years. "Let's get a national survey done right away to establish a baseline. N of 1200. Then let's do pairs of groups in Budapest and two other locations. Jason, what do you suggest?"

Jason called up Hungary on Google maps on his computer and projected it on a screen at the end of the conference table. "Well, Fidesz has a pretty good stronghold on the entire country. Our guy doesn't really have any kind of a support base outside of Budapest, so we can go anywhere."

"I suggest we do Debrecen out east and Szegeg in the south," Lisa said, walking up to the map and pointing at the locations with her pen. "That gives us geographic diversity, and we can split the groups by age and gender. We then drill down to see what's driving likely voters in each subgroup. We build a mobilization strategy based on what the data tell us. Given that they were the two strongest groups for our guy last time around, I think it gives us a good place to start."

"David?" Miles asked.

David nodded and scrunched his nose, though he loathed giving Lisa credit. Those were the same cities and target groups he was planning to recommend, but she jumped on the opportunity first.

Lisa sat down and leaned forward in her chair, squeezing her chest together slightly and winking at him. David shifted in his seat.

"So, once we establish the baseline and filter through the focus group results," David continued, "we can get a better idea of where we should do additional targeted polling and the next round of groups."

A knock on the door preceded Margaret's head popping through. "Henry just called, Mr. Davis. Hungary is an official go."

"He confirmed the money's in the account?" Miles asked.

"Yes. The wire just came through—$1.5 million."

David whistled.

"Good, then. All right, kids, you know what to do. Lisa, I want you to come, too."

"What? I have a meeting with the Nigerians tomorrow."

"Screw the Nigerians. They're just gonna jerk us around. Send Patrick. Hungary's real, and it's happening. I want you there on the ground with us. Plus, that way, we can split groups. After Budapest, you can do one city and Dave can do the other. That allows me to stay in the capital and work with all the different pieces on this to bring everyone together."

"OK." Lisa unconsciously glanced at David, catching his eye for a moment before he turned to Miles.

"So, we go through Frankfurt?" David asked.

"Ugh. I guess so. Frankfurt, it is, goddamn it."

CHAPTER TWO

"No sé, mi amor," Cecilia said, sitting on the stool at the end of their bed. She stared out through the open balcony door overlooking Barranquilla, the city where she grew up. Muggy humidity coated everything. The strength of the day's heat that baked into the streets and sidewalks held the city in a vise grip. As night descended, however, the soothing Caribbean breeze moved in, providing the city with much needed relief. Above, the moonlight hid most of the stars, but a few were strong enough to make their presence known. The soft glow of the corner floor lamp cast hazy shadows around the room. She gulped the last of her wine and looked at her husband, knowing he had already made up his mind. Regardless, she didn't have the strength to fight him any longer. Her head felt dizzy from the alcohol.

"Es que tengo que hacerlo, Cecilia, y tu lo sabes," Enrique said. "It's that I have to do this, and you know it."

"Pero mi padre..." Emotions welled in her chest, and she feared she wouldn't be able to hold them down. It was still too raw, too close to home, even though if felt like four lifetimes ago.

"I'm not your father. The same thing won't happen to me. I promise."

"How can you promise me that?" The floodgates she feared wouldn't hold suddenly broke, and out it came. "Tell me! How? These people are crazy and will do anything to stop you from winning. They don't care about anything else. If you stand in their way, they'll shoot you like a dog that needs to be put down. I just couldn't see you..." Sobs took over, and she couldn't continue.

"Venga, mi amor," he said, clutching her arms and setting his chin on top her head.

He recalled the day her father was shot. It was a Saturday in summer, well before he met her at the corner café, the same one where her parents had met, as she told him. He remembered the unbearable heat, similar to today's scorcher.

He held his mother's leg to stay under the shadow of her umbrella. Body odor permeated the crowd, mixing with his mom's perfume and the wild cheers that went up when he came out onto the veranda.

Then there was a loud pop, followed by several more, and panic. The entire crowd in the plaza fell like an invisible hand had smashed them all down. His mother lay atop him, screaming. He scraped his knee.

"I just..." Cecilia said, unable to get the rest of the words out.

"I know, my love, but the time is right. The time for me is now. This country needs change, and I can bring that change. The people need me."

"I need you."

Enrique Arenas kissed her forehead and walked to the bar to pour a scotch, an Ardbeg single-malt, fifteen years old—his favorite. He remembered the first time he drank it, he almost gagged. The peaty intensity was something he had never experienced before. Now he looked forward to his nightly scotch almost as much as anything else in his life.

He unfastened the cufflinks from his shirt and set them beside the cup. From the icebox, he took a small spoonful of cold water and dumped it into the whiskey glass. The small drops of water really opened up the whiskey, he'd been taught.

He sniffed and took a sip, savoring the alcohol's teeth biting into the back of his throat. A car alarm broke the silence for a few seconds, then went off, followed by the bark of a distant dog. He stared blankly out the veranda door.

"Alfredo knows a gringo in DC. He says he's the best with campaigns. He can help us win."

"Can he make sure you don't get killed?"

"*Amor, por favor...*"

Cecilia got up and walked onto the balcony, crying freely, as mascara blotted the corner of her eyes. Nothing he could say or do would calm her fears. They had to go through this together, and he knew she'd be sick with worry the entire time. Her mother became catatonic after her husband's assassination. She spent her days staring out the window of her nursing home, mumbling incoherently under her breath.

"I don't want to become my mother, Enrique." Cecilia leaned against the balcony rail, inhaling the night air deep into her lungs.

"I don't want you to, either, my love." Enrique walked up behind her and embraced her waist. Sweat beaded on his upper lip. He was equally nervous and excited about his decision, though he couldn't tell which his wife had seen on his face. He put his chin on her shoulder as they both stared out into nothing.

It was a muggy night.

CHAPTER THREE

I hate pundits. Goddamn bloodsucking leaches who feed off partisan strife. They're the only ones who benefit when this town is gridlocked. Them and the lobbyists. They get on TV and bloviate on talking points handed down to them from on high. Here, Douchebag, go and blabber about these points, because that's the news cycle for the day, and because the clowns down the street are sending their Douchebag to yap, so you must go. I wish we could herd all of them into Canada.

"And welcome back," the host said. "We're excited to have with us in the studio Mr. Miles Davis, President and CEO of Verge Consulting. Known as the Kingmaker, he's a world-renowned political consultant and strategist, having won campaigns in the United States and around the world for the past two decades. He recently released a book with the same title, *Kingmaker,* which details his political exploits.

"He has a Master's degree from Harvard in Political Science and is fluent in Spanish, French, Arabic, and Japanese, with a couple others, as well. I hope you don't mind if I conduct this interview in English, Mr. Davis?"

"Of course." *Jackass.*

The host laughed. "Great. Mr. Davis is just coming off another election in Hungary, where he helped guide the opposition candidate to a stunning victory over the Prime

Minister and his party. We'll definitely dig into that feat on today's show, as well as others that have grabbed headlines over the last few years. First, Mr. Davis, welcome."

"Good to be here, Anderson. And please, call me Miles."

"Very well, Miles. So, tell us, how do you do what you do?"

"You might not believe me, Anderson, but it's not rocket science. The goal of all elections is to win one more vote than the other guy or party. Of course, each country is different, and there are differences from election to election, too, but it basically breaks down like this.

"You have hard-core supporters on either side, or a couple of sides if you're dealing with parliamentary elections, whom you'll never convince no matter what you do or say to change sides. Then there are the folks in the middle, the swing voters, who can be convinced one way or the other. You have to identify who those people are and where they live.

"Next comes teasing out what's important to those people. What are they concerned about? What would motivate them to get out and vote? Develop a strategy of explaining to those people why your guy will address those concerns better than the other guy. Then you ensure they get out and vote on election day."

"Sound easy."

"Yes. I told you, it's not rocket science."

"Some people say, however, that you do have this kind of work down to a science."

"Well, a lot of what we do is scientific in a way. How we conduct polling, for example, or how we set up focus groups and test messages. Those things are pretty scientific in the sense that we've done them so many times that we know exactly how to do them. It's also important to have an incredible staff working with you, because it's what you do with that information and how you apply it to the context where you're working that makes the difference. Anyone can conduct a poll and do focus groups, Anderson, but not everyone can do what my team and I can with that information."

"That's what makes you the Kingmaker."

Miles couldn't help smiling. He loved that nickname.

CHAPTER FOUR

"Boss, did you see the *Miami Herald* today?" David asked, walking into Miles' office and sliding his iPad across the desk.

"Maybe. Why?"

"Enrique just declared he's running in Colombia."

"Yeah. I knew it last week."

"Well, shit. How'd you know that?"

"Alfredo."

"Alfredo? *The* Alfredo?"

"Yes, my boy—Alfredo Di Stefano."

"I thought after Chile we were done with Freddy."

"Bygones, David. We can't hold grudges. It just makes your ass pucker up and adds lines to your face. Unbecoming, I must say."

"Yeah, but..."

"But nothing. What happened in Chile happened. Get over it. Freddy knows Enrique and says he's the Colombian Nelson Mandela. He's the bright new face in Colombian politics. He'll help defeat the drug cartels. He'll bring peace and prosperity to the country."

"Already writing the talking points, eh?"

"Always, my boy." Mile grinned.

"He's married to Galan's daughter, right?"

"Yes, he is. Cecilia Galan. Freddy says she's strongly against his running."

"I don't blame her after what happened to her father."

"Yeah, I agree, but that's a hurdle we'll have to jump sooner rather than later, and we have to be delicate about it. The sooner she's onboard, the better we'll be, and the better Enrique can focus on his campaign and win it."

"You think he has a chance?"

"Doesn't matter what I think. The only thing that matters is that he believes he can win, and that he *wants* to win. If his wife isn't one-hundred percent behind him, it'll show in him, and that's bad."

"Agree. So, what's the plan? Are we jumping on the campaign?"

"Not sure yet. I spoke only briefly to Freddy on the phone. I said we wouldn't mind having a chat, and he said he'd fly up to meet us. He'll be here any minute."

"Oh. OK." David walked to the wet bar and cappuccino machine. Taking out a cup and saucer, he held them under the spout and pressed the espresso button. Steamy milk poured from the pipe, followed by a slow drip of dark, hot coffee.

"Fucking Freddy," David muttered, thinking back to Santiago and the last time he saw the man, when they shared an awkward, melancholy handshake at the airport.

Safe travels, Guys.

Yeah. Thanks. Keep in touch.

Sure.

"You want one?" David asked Miles.

"No. I'm good." Miles picked up the newspaper and continued reading where he left off. David added two packets of sugar to his cup and moved to the window with the view of the Capitol.

"This view never gets old," he said.

"No, it doesn't."

"Have they said how long the renovations will take?"

Before Miles could reply, someone knocked on the door, then Margaret came in. "Mr. Davis, Alfredo Di Stefano is here to see you."

"Send him in, Margaret." After she left, he said, "Maybe a year? Two?"

"That long?" David stirred his espresso with a wooden stick and tossed it into the garbage. For some reason, the scaffolding outside reminded him of the Egyptian pyramids.

Did they use a similar construction method? he wondered.

A minute later, another knock on the door announced Alfredo's arrival. A heavyset man in his late sixties, he had thinning salt-and-pepper hair and a clean-shaven face, bottomed out by a good-sized double chin. Fat black eyes stared from his face, and his gaze seemed directed by his pointed nose. Three gold chains hung from his neck into the black-and-white chest hair pouring from his open-collared dress shirt. The scent of strong cologne filled the room.

"*Señor Di Stefano.*" Miles walked around his desk and warmly embraced the man. They patted each other's backs like old friends and held each other at arm's length.

David almost saw them taking the measure of each other. It had been years since all three of them were in the same room—not since Santiago.

"*Señor Davis*, it's so good to see you. Thank you for taking my call last week and for meeting me today." Alfredo's heavily accented English was carried melodically on the shoulders of his baritone voice.

"No worries, Freddy. You remember David Strasbourg, yes? He was in Chile with us."

"Yes, of course I do. How are you, Mr. David?"

"I'm great, Mr. Di Stefano. It's good to see you again."

"How is your wife?"

"Good, good. Thank you." David was surprised that Alfredo remembered he was married.

"Any *hijos* yet?"

"Yes, a two-year-old and another on the way."

"Congratulations! That's very nice to hear. Please give my

regards to your family."

"I will, Mr. Di Stefano."

"Please. I tell you before, call me Alfredo, or Freddy, like Mr. Davis. I like when he calls me Freddy."

"And I've told you before to call me Miles."

"*Por supuesto,* Miles." Alfredo returned the smile.

Miles motioned toward the sofa chairs near the window with the view of the Capitol. They each took a single chair, while David sat on the long sofa, pulling the lid off his pen and flipping to a clean page in his notebook.

"So, Miles, have you decided to follow David and calm your horses to settle down with a good woman?" Alfredo asked, winking at David.

"I found one but forgot her at the train station."

They laughed.

"How about you?" Miles asked. "How are things with Esmeralda and the girls?"

"They're good. *Gracias,* Miles. Esmeralda is always bothering me about my weight. She has the girls in a conspiracy with her against me, I tell you. It's a fight to feed me vegetables, but I won't give in!"

All three laughed.

"Can I get you coffee or water?" David asked, realizing he'd been remiss.

"*Un cortado* would be great, David. *Gracias.*"

David got up and walked back to the wet bar. Alfredo took out a pack of cigarettes from his pocket and looked inquiringly at Miles, who nodded.

"I also have to sneak my tobacco these days," Alfredo admitted.

David, hearing a lighter ignite, reached under the cabinet drawer for an ashtray.

Alfredo took a deep drag on his cigarette and turned his gaze to David, then Miles. Miles knew he was weighing what words he would use and purposefully let the pause lengthen, so Alfredo would speak first.

"*Señor* Miles, before we start, about Chile. I'm so sorry."

Before he could continue, Miles raised his hand. "Freddy, please. You don't have to apologize. It wasn't your fault. Shit happens. We're good."

"We're good?"

"Yes."

"OK, *muy bueno entonces.* Anyways, I will never forgive myself for getting us into that *mierda. Qué hijo de puta!* I'm glad you are OK now."

"Yes. David and I are fine."

They glanced at David, who nodded.

Sure, David thought. *It's not like I wasted a year of my life working for a candidate who ended up being charged with corruption and then confirmed the charges by fleeing to Cuba with all the remaining campaign money and his mistress one week before the election.*

"Excellent," Alfredo said. "Let's talk about what we discussed briefly on the phone last week."

"Yes, let's."

"Enrique Arenas, the future of our country. I'm here to ask for your services in helping me get him elected as the next President of Colombia."

"That sounds great, Freddy, but I'm concerned about Enrique."

"*Por qué?*"

"Well, a couple of reasons. First, he's a novice. He comes from a good, well-connected family, yes, but he hasn't done anything political."

"*Sí, pero* he successfully built his business from scratch. It's a multimillion-dollar enterprise that provides thousands of jobs. His favorables are already very high."

"I know his résumé, Freddy. He's a successful businessman, and that would be the major card we play in the campaign, but he hasn't held political office before. Why is he going for president and not senator?"

"Because it's the right moment for him and for our country. Yes, he lacks the political experience, but he has incredibly good experience in other areas. He's ready to do this. The other candidates are a bunch of *pendejos* who can be defeated if we have a focused, professionally run campaign. He needs a *Señor* Miles-led campaign."

Alfredo knew how much Miles liked having his ego stroked, and he wasn't about to hold back. He couldn't imagine returning to Bogota without Miles and his team onboard.

"I'm also worried about Cecilia."

"Don't be." Alfredo took a final drag of his cigarette and put it out in the ashtray. "I spoke to Enrique last week before I called you. He said they had a conversation, and she's behind him."

"One hundred percent?"

"Cien porciento."

"She can fuck everything up, Freddy. You know that."

"Sí, pero she is also our trump card. She's young and beautiful, as well as smart and very charming. The camera loves her. Of course, everyone knows her story and what happened to her papa." He unconsciously touched his left shoulder where a bullet hit him that day. He'd been her father's campaign manager during that election and stood on the veranda with him on that hot summer's day. He was shot by the same gunmen who killed her father. Every day, he wondered why God hadn't taken him as well, or instead of, Cecilia's father.

He would have been a great president, Alfredo thought sadly. *Why did He spare me and not Luis Carlos?*

That thought bothered him more than it consoled him.

"They can be our John and Jackie Kennedy."

"That's a lofty ambition," Miles said.

"Come to Bogota and meet him, and then make up your

mind."

Miles walked to the window facing the Capitol. By the way he tapped his fingers on his crossed elbows, David knew he had already made up his mind. He'd been in this exact situation with Miles countless times. Miles couldn't wait to start work on that campaign. What was not to like? It involved a young, smart, sexy, rising star in Latin American politics with a gorgeous wife, facing a field of weak candidates and an even weaker incumbent. F.A.R.C. was fracturing and was a shell of its former self, on the brink of making a peace deal. Colombia was a country on the rise with a youthful, energetic population that was dying for a chance at a better life that all knew they could have if they only had the right leader to show them the way to the promised land. The country was like a ripe piece of fruit—all it needed was the right hand, guided by a skilled professional, to harvest it.

However, at that precise moment in a seventh-floor corner office in a building only a three-iron away from the White House, it was time to get paid.

"I don't know, Freddy," Miles said.

"Come on, Miles. If it's money you're worried about, or getting paid, don't have any fear. I have the campaign funds under my control. I have my laptop with me. I can wire money into your account immediately. Enrique gave me permission to spend what I need to get you onboard."

"It's not the money, Freddy," Mile said, moving in for the kill. "It's working for someone people can truly believe in. Do you really think he's up for it? As a Colombian, do *you* believe in him?"

Alfredo sat up straight, fighting the lump in his throat. "With everything I've got. He'll do what those bastard assassins didn't let Luis Carlos do."

Miles gave him a hard look. "Three million. Half now, half one month before the election. No exceptions. My team starts immediately. We're in charge of everything. I bring in who I want when I want. If I tell him or you to jump, your only reply is, 'How high?'"

"Deal."

"Great." He was a bit shocked at how easy it was. He expected Freddy to hem and haw over the price and felt slightly disappointed that he hadn't. "David will get the contract written up and sent over for signature."

All three stood to shake hands. Alfredo had a big smile. David couldn't believe they just shook on a three-million-dollar contract.

"I'm in town for a couple more days," Alfredo said. "Have the paperwork sent to my hotel. I'll wire you the money this afternoon." He walked toward the door.

"Freddy, one last thing," Miles said. "How high would you have gone?"

Alfredo smiled. "Four." He winked at David. "How low would you have gone?"

"Two."

They all laughed.

Chapter Five

I really don't like homeless people. I know most have been dealt terrible hands in the game of life, but Man, I can't get over the fact that they're such a freaking eyesore. Sweet Jesus, the smell is unbearable! This entire freaking town is crawling with them—metro entrances, street corners, park benches, everywhere! And what's up with the guys who are always in the same location? I've seen the same guy on the same corner for the past ten years. They must be making money, or they wouldn't be there, I guess. I would think that if they stand in the same place all the time, the same people would walk past them more often than not, no? They might offer some change occasionally, but more than once? Wouldn't it be a better strategy for them to rotate locations that would capitalize on the first sympathetic reactions with new, never-before-seen individuals? Do bums have turf wars?

McPherson Square is located a few hundred feet from the White House in Washington, DC. It isn't famous for its statue of unknown Union General James B. McPherson, erected by the Society of the Army of the Tennessee on October 18, 1876, but rather for the vagrant and olfactory-assaulting homeless population that live in and around the square.

Miles found an unoccupied bench near the center. The smell of one of the homeless men sleeping on a nearby bench felt like it permeated the entire block, or was that just the general stench in the air? He couldn't tell, but wherever it came from, it was unpleasant.

He glanced at his watch. It was 10:03 AM.

A man in a black suit and black tie with beige trench coat approached the bench and sat beside Miles. He was tall and broad shouldered, with a thick neck, clean-cut face, and a cut jaw line. His gait betrayed a military background, while his clothes indicated he was employed by the federal government. Force of habit made him glance around to ensure no one was within hearing distance.

"Hey, there, Miles. Good to see you again."

"Hey, John. Yes. Not since Yemen. What can I do for you, John?" He didn't like John Carpenter much. It wasn't the man he disliked, per se. For all Miles knew, he paid his taxes on time, was nice to his wife and kids, and didn't drink and drive. No, what held John Carpenter low on Miles' list of people was due to John's current employer and the debt he knew he would one day have to repay. John worked for the CIA, and that agency saved Miles' life a few years earlier in Yemen. Miles had been in Sana'a and was scheduled to meet with a Saudi prince who was interested in diversifying his billions into infrastructure projects in Central America. Miles had worked on the campaigns of the sitting presidents in Panama, Costa Rica, and El Salvador.

It was a typical meeting that Miles had every month, for which he requested only a modest fee of $10,000 and all expenses paid. Most of the people he made connections for and with had no problem paying that amount, because the deals they often struck made Miles' fee look like a single grain of sand in a sandbox.

John stood near the hotel lobby entrance, doing a poor job of hiding behind a newspaper. As Miles walked past to flag a taxi, John said to Miles, "I wouldn't go to your meeting if I were you."

"Excuse me?"

John lowered the newspaper. "I would advise you to miss

this meeting with Sheikh Mohammed Abdullah, Miles."

Miles, a bit unnerved, looked around the lobby. "Do I know you?"

"No, but I know you. Let's head to the bar, OK? I'll explain."

"Look, I don't know who you are or what you want, but I was paid to fly 7,000 miles for this meeting, and I'm not going to miss it just because some crackpot in the hotel lobby says so."

"Miles," John said, lowering his voice, "there will be an attempt to kidnap Sheikh Mohammed Abdullah this afternoon."

"What? How do you know?"

"Please. I insist. Come to the bar with me, and I'll explain everything."

At the bar, John said he worked for the CIA, which had solid evidence that the kidnapping would take place that afternoon. Then he laid out the details behind it. It was being staged by Yemeni Houthi rebels in an attempt to blackmail the Saudi government to pull out of Yemeni affairs. Their plan was to use a road blockade.

He gave enough of an explanation and in such a way that Miles was convinced to postpone the meeting. He called the Prince's handlers and asked to reschedule for the following day. They promised to call back later in the day. They never did.

In the evening, the news reported that the kidnapping had been attempted, only to go completely haywire. When it was over, the Prince, four bodyguards, all five kidnappers, and two policemen were dead.

John met a shell-shocked Miles at the hotel restaurant later that evening and asked if it was all right if they stayed in touch. Miles agreed.

Miles took a plane back to DC the following morning. Since then, he felt indebted to the Agency and John for warning him, and he hated the feeling that he owed something to someone. They would ask to be repaid someday, which meant they would probably want access to his work, Miles surmised. The entire thing smelled like a setup, though even Miles at his most cynical couldn't imagine it had been.

The meeting in McPherson Square was the first time he'd seen John since Sana'a.

"Straight to business. All right, then," John said. "Enrique Arenas."

"What about him?"

"We hear you're going to work on his campaign."

"I guess it would be pointless for me to deny it."

"Correct. We would be grateful if you would keep us apprised of what he's thinking and doing—and what his policies would look like if he were elected."

"What do you mean, apprised?"

"You know. Just keep us informed about where he would take the country in the eventuality of his becoming president. I don't have to tell you that the Agency has a keen interest in Colombia."

"So, you've finally come to collect for saving me."

"Now, don't be crass, Miles. We'd never think of it like that."

"I'm surprised you haven't reached out earlier, like maybe to check and see if I was doing OK after Yemen."

"We knew you were OK."

"Of course, you did. Are we done?"

"Yes. Thanks, Miles. I'll be in touch from time to time."

"Yeah, sure."

John stood and walked away. The homeless guy on the bench raised his head and mumbled something incoherent to John, then laid his head down again. Miles walked in the opposite direction towards his office, muttering obscenities under his breath.

Chapter Six

Lisa: Yo dude, where you at?
David: Still at the office.
Lisa: C'mon. A few of us are at Churchkey. You should come.
David: No, I can't. The wifey is waiting for me at home.
Lisa: Loser.
Lisa: Jk! Gosh...
Lisa: One beer won't kill you, will it?
David: Fine. Be there in 10 min.

David found Lisa, Jason, and Sarah at a booth in the back of ChurchKey, a dimly lit, second-floor bar on the 14th Street NW corridor with a great selection of microbrew draft beers. Happy hour just started, but the bar was still half-empty. Lisa, seeing David walking through the bar, raised her hand.

"Hey, y'all, he made it!" Sarah Larson, one of the analysts at Verge, said. Skinny and blonde, she sported a pink sweater and form-fitting navy-blue plants. She normally wore her hair in a loose ponytail that hung past her shoulders. Her looks and easy Southern charm belied a ruthless political instinct that made her a valuable asset. She was the company's communications guru, and the team relied on her ability to distill the mounds of data from their research into simple, easily digestible talking points. She hid her southern North Carolina roots well, but the twang came out at times after a few drinks. She was Lisa's best friend.

"Yeah, yeah," David said. "Only one beer. I can't stay long. Gotta get home soon."

"For the wifey," Lisa teased.

David raised a finger to his lips while motioning her to scoot over.

"So, David, what do you think about Colombia?" Jason asked. He wasn't known for talking about much other than work.

"I like it. I think we have a great candidate and optimum conditions for victory."

"You aren't concerned about his, you know, lack of political experience?" Sarah asked.

"Yeah, it's a concern, but shit. Remember Funes?"

"That's right," Jason chimed in. "He had no political experience before winning the presidency."

"He was a TV personality and a journalist," Lisa countered. "He had name recognition. And I worked that campaign. That's why he won."

Everyone laughed.

"Of course, it is," David said. "Not that any of us who also worked on that campaign had anything to do with it." He poked her ribs with an elbow and smiled, and she playfully pushed back.

"Look," David continued, "Miles is confident we can set him up to be the clear choice to move Colombia forward. He doesn't have any political baggage that the other candidates do. He's young, good-looking, and has some pretty good ideas. Alfredo sent through his platform pillars, and they're strong. Of course, we'll have to see how the likelies react, but I think, all in all, he's on the right track."

"And with Verge Consulting pulling the strings behind the curtain," Sarah said, raising her glass for a toast.

Jason mimicked a puppeteer, and the others laughed.

"To Colombia and to Enrique Arenas! *Salud!*"

They touched glasses.

"All right." Sarah finished her beer and set down a ten-dollar bill. "I have to go. See y'all tomorrow." She lingered for a second, giving Jason a quick glance, thinking no one noticed, but David caught it.

The others said, "'Bye," except Jason, who smiled into his beer.

After she left, David said, "He still hasn't done it, has he?"

"Nope." Lisa grinned with David as Jason moped over his beer.

Feeling their stares, he looked up. "What?"

"Nothing!" they said.

"You mean why haven't I asked her out yet? Because I'm smart enough to know she'd never go for me."

"You'll never know unless you jump," Lisa said.

Jason suddenly sat up straight. "What? Do you know something?"

Lisa gave him a coy smile and winked at David.

"Come on," Jason begged. "What?"

"Let's just say that if I were you, I'd ask her out."

"Really?"

"Yes."

Jason's eyes widened. He smiled and thought hard for a moment, looking at David as if searching for confirmation. David pursed his lips and gave a single sharp nod.

That was all Jason needed. He took one last swig of his beer, dropped a five-dollar bill on the table, and went after Sarah.

"Why does he still think a beer in this city costs only five dollars?" Lisa asked.

"I'll cover him." David pocketed the money.

Neither David nor Lisa expected to be left alone together. Not wanting the awkwardness to grow, she blurted the first question that came to mind.

"Are you truly excited about Colombia?"

"Yeah. Another gig, right?"

"Yeah. Will Miles let you take the lead on this one?"

"I think so, though I know he'll be heavily involved, at least at the beginning."

"How long have you guys known each other?"

"Over twenty years." His memory riffled through all he'd done with Miles: the campaigns, the crazy hours and travel, the women...

"He's the one who gave me my first chance to prove myself."

"Would you ever want to work for someone else?"

"I don't know if I could. Maybe for myself someday, but not for someone else."

"He's like a father to you."

"You could say that. I didn't know my own dad very well. He left my mother when I was five, and I've spoken to him only a couple times since. To be honest, I don't care too much for him. Miles took me under his wing. The rest, as they say, is history."

"What's your favorite Miles story?"

David laughed and finished off his beer. As was his wont, he finished his first beer quickly. When he drank, he usually ramped up fast. As he signaled the waiter for a refill, Lisa smiled.

"Shit. Let's see," David said, rubbing his hand through his hair. "Where to start?" He dug through his memory. "Oh, yeah. Definitely Romania in the late '90s. It was one of our first international campaigns. We were doing groups in Bucharest, if I remember correctly. Afterward, we went out for dinner. Our translator took us to a really nice place, and we had a fantastic meal.

"As we were wrapping up, I thought we'd head back to the hotel. We had to get up early and drive to another city for groups there, but Miles grabbed the translator's arm and asked him in a *faux* serious tone, 'Where do true, salt-of-the-earth

Romanians get drinks around here?' The translator thought he meant girls, but Miles just wanted drinks. He wanted to leave the tourist area and hit the town local style."

"He loves doing that, doesn't he?"

"Definitely. You know what his two criteria are for officially considering having been somewhere?"

"No."

"The first one is rather gross. It's taking a number two."

"Gross!" She laughed.

"Told you! And the second is having a local beer, preferably in a local watering hole, but it must be local beer. If he hasn't done both, he doesn't include the country in his country count."

"How many has he been to?"

"Countries?" David sipped from his larger beer, while Lisa asked the waiter for another. "Shit, it must be over a hundred."

"You?"

"Seventy-three. You?"

"Fifty-eight."

They smiled, happy they knew their country counts without thinking, and content to be in company where throwing out their respective numbers wasn't seen as bragging. Most of their friends and acquaintances were in the single digits, if they knew at all. Some didn't even have passports. Saying you'd been to that many countries never sounded right when said aloud.

They held a pause in their conversation for a moment, happy to be in each other's company outside work.

"Anyway," she said, "Romania. Salt of the earth locals."

"Oh, yeah. So, our translator—I can't remember his name, Silvain or something like it—he'd been with us a couple days by then and got to know us and what Miles liked. We jumped into a cab and left the city, pulling up at a place that sat beside the road. It was a big wooden structure that looked like half a house and half a restaurant.

"Everything inside was wood, including the chairs, tables, and walls. The place hummed with locals. It was clearly a popular spot. A big hearth on one side had a raging fire. It was November, so it was freezing. We saddled up to a picnic-style table and bench near the fire. Miles asked Silvain what real Romanians drank. He said, '*Tuica.*' Miles said we should get a bottle. Silvain flagged down a waitress, and she came back a few minutes later with a big bottle and three shot glasses."

"I can see where this is going," Lisa mused.

"No, it's not what you think. We started downing shot after shot. It's a liquor made from plums, a little sweet with a nice kick to it. After a couple shots, I was getting pretty sauced, but Miles and the translator kept drinking them down. Miles seems to get sharper when he drinks."

"I agree." Lisa laughed.

"So, at some point, the translator looks to another table and leans over in a conspiratorial manner. He says that the group at the table over there are the campaign manager and senior team of the guy we were running against."

"No way!"

"Yes. So, Miles concocted a plan to start talking with them. He told the translator to say he was an American researcher writing a book about new democratic movements across Eastern Europe, and he would be interested in hearing how they're running their campaign. In exchange for sharing their stories, Miles offered to buy them all the booze they wanted.

"Of course, they were more than happy to exchange what they knew to some random American for free booze. After moving over to our table and drinking a couple of bottles, they spilled their entire campaign strategy to us."

"No shit? That's crazy."

"Right!? They told us about the opposition research they had on our guy, what they were worried about in our candidate, the works. We had their entire playbook. It wasn't even fair. After we won the election, Miles sent the manager a thank-you card with a picture of us and our candidate."

"That's hilarious."

"It was awesome. That was the campaign where I first realized I wanted to do this for the rest of my life." He took a big swig from his beer and let out a big sigh.

"Yeah. Experiences like that will do that to you."

"What about you?"

"Hmmm. Let me think." Glancing at her watch, she saw it was ten minutes past the time David said he could stay. For the first time, she wondered what it would be like to kiss him, and that startled her. She shook her head to dismiss the thought.

David noticed. "You OK?"

"Yeah." *Perceptive fucker,* she thought. "Just trying to think of a good Miles story." She took another sip of her beer.

"OK I've got one. We were coming back to DC from New York one day two years ago, and he wanted to stop in Baltimore at a sandwich shop. He said they had the best crab-cake sandwiches.

"We found the place and went inside to eat. The sandwiches really were freaking good. As we left, we saw at the end of the street what seemed like the beginning of a parade, so we looked at each other and silently agreed to check it out. They were setting up a small plaza where they were about to dedicate a memorial to the Katyn massacre of World War Two."

"The one where the Russians killed all those Polish army officers?"

"Yeah. From the crowd, it looked like a serious affair. Then out of nowhere, someone called Miles' name with a thick Polish accent. Would you believe it was freaking Milosz?" She sipped from her beer, starting to feel the effects.

She realized she hadn't eaten anything, which explained it.

"No shit!"

"Yeah! So, Milosz comes over and says the Prime Minister and everyone was there and asked what we were doing there. We said we were driving through and stumbled on the place. He said that was great and invited us to be part of the ceremony and wreath laying.

"Of course, Miles agreed. He's always in his suit, so he pulled a tie from his pocket and was ready to go with Milosz to where the Prime Minister was with the rest of his delegation. Would you believe he sat up in the front row with the Poles, then he walked arm-in-arm with everyone else to place wreaths on the memorial?"

"That's hilarious."

"I couldn't believe it."

"Yeah, that's classic Miles."

"Yup."

They both sipped their drinks.

I wonder what she's like in bed, David thought, surprised that popped into his head. He always had a natural, man-to-woman attraction to Lisa, but work always came first for both of them. She was the best coworker he'd ever had. He knew Miles valued her as much as he valued him. Their professional work barrier held for the four years they had worked together. He'd never thought of her sexually until that moment.

Could be spurred by the problems I'm having at home with Stacy, he thought. *We haven't had sex in two months.*

"So how are things at home?" Lisa asked, as if reading David's thoughts.

He looked at her in surprise. "Good! Good."

"Great." She silently rebuked herself for asking in such a stupid way.

"Well, yeah, things could be better, I guess. I don't know." He felt uncomfortable discussing his home life, especially with Lisa. He'd been married for over a decade, but the love in the marriage had been leaking like a sieve for the past couple of years. He still loved his wife, but it was more of an appreciation for having a life partner, someone to share a home with and raise kids together. They were comfortable, and he was grateful. She was an excellent mother, and he knew she loved him deeply.

From the outside, they had a perfect, enviable life. The passion, however, was gone. It had been for a while, but recently, it felt more poignant. The butterflies in the stomach, the sweaty palms, the knot in the throat he had for his wife from the moment he first saw her at a drunken college frat party so many years in the past—those feelings had vacated his heart for some time. He had grown as a man and an individual over the last ten years. He wasn't the same person he'd been in his early twenties. The thought constantly nagged at him, and he didn't know what it meant.

"What do you mean?" she asked.

"Oh, nothing. Stacy and I are just going through some shit. I'd rather not talk about it, frankly. And you? How's Scott?"

"You mean Stewart?"

"Yeah. Sorry. When's the wedding?"

"We haven't set a date yet. He's pretty hard-headed at times. He's waiting for a promotion and feels he needs to secure that before we can get married. He thinks he's inadequate right now in terms of his income to marry me. I tell him it's ridiculous, but he needs to have things done his way in a specific, particular manner. Promotion first, marriage second."

"Do you think you guys will have kids?" He was halfway done with his second beer.

"Yes, of course. Well, I mean, I want to."

"What about him?"

"Yes. Well, I think so."

David raised an eyebrow. "Don't you think that's something you should be sure of before you tie the knot?"

"He said he's open to the possibility."

"Open to the possibility?"

Lisa looked away and drank her beer, realizing the string she hung her familial hopes on was more precarious than she thought. David saw her turning morose and glanced at his watch, seeing how late it was.

"Shit," he said. "I'd better head home." He chugged the rest of his beer.

"Yeah, me, too."

"That was fun. Thanks for dragging me out for a few beers. We should do it more often."

"Yeah. That sounds great."

"All right." He set money on the table to cover his drinks and Jason's. "You OK sticking behind to close out the tab?"

"Yeah, of course."

"Great. Well, good night, Lisa." He held her gaze for a split second longer than intended, caught in that awkward pause that lingers when work colleagues have to say good-bye to each other in a social setting. *Should I hug her? Kiss her cheek?* He opted for neither.

"Good night, David." She stared at his behind until he disappeared down the stairs.

I really do wonder how he kisses...

CHAPTER SEVEN

The only redeeming quality Brussels has is its proximity to better cities in Europe, like London, Paris, and Amsterdam. What a characterless, bureaucratic shithole. The old town has its cute streets and a certain charm, but the rest of the town sucks. Why would anyone want to live there unless you were so unfortunate to be born Belgian, or your life had taken an ill-fated turn into becoming a Eurocrat? Or visit, for that matter, when there are so many better places to see? Oh, that's right. The Europeans, in all their genius, put the center of European politics here. It's like giving the ugly girl in school the Miss Congeniality prize, so she won't cry. Paris can't have everything, I guess.

The taxi circled past the European Parliament and went north down Rue Wiertz. It was a starless night, and a slight mist hung in the air. A mischievous breeze made the weather colder than it should have been, forcing pedestrians to hold up their coat collars to protect their faces from the chilly Brussels night. Miles pulled his directionless gaze from the passersby outside the cab and touched the side of his iPhone to check the time. It was 9:38 PM.

She said the reservation was for 9:45, he thought.

"*Oui c'est restaurant, Monsieur?*" The cabbie asked.

"*Comme Chez Soi, c'est ici.*" Miles said before it came into view.

Comme Chez Soi was one of Belgium's most-famous restaurants. Tucked away in a townhouse beside a chain pastry shop, it didn't look like much from the outside, but it was Michelin starred for years and was Miles' favorite place in the city. The ability to have dinner at the Comme Chez Soi made a trip to Brussels worth it.

That's probably why she chose it.

After checking his coat with the maître d', he said, "I'm expecting someone here for a dinner reservation for two."

"I believe she's already here," the maître d' said. "Around the corner, window table."

Miles went down the short hall and turned the corner leading back toward the front of the restaurant. There she was, sitting in a corner at a table for two, a glass of red wine in her hand. The small room barely fit six tables in its tight confines. It was dim with candle sconces hanging from the walls on both sides, giving the room a romantic glow. White linens covered the tables, and, other than a group of four a few tables down, who appeared to be finishing their meal, and a couple sitting at the table beside theirs, the restaurant was empty.

Interesting for a Friday night. He recalled the recent terrorist attacks at the airport and in the subway.

That's probably kept many people away.

Lauren Bastille was gorgeous by any definition of the word. Tall, slim, with blonde hair hanging loosely past her shoulders, she had perpetually sad, blue, puppy-dog eyes. Her thick lips formed a natural pout, giving the appearance that she either wanted to start bawling or make out passionately; Miles could never tell which. Her long, red dress fit her slender body and small breasts perfectly. Black high heels and a gold necklace with a single diamond hanging from it and matching earrings completed her outfit. Some of her red lipstick smudged the wine glass before her. Light crow's feet hugged the sides of her eyes, but the forty-three-year-old could easily pass for someone in her late twenties.

Miles was a lifelong bachelor. The closest he ever came to settling down was in his early twenties with Lauren, with whom he had shared an apartment in Madrid. Theirs was a passionate love affair. She wanted him to move back to Paris with her when school finished. Everything was set, but the morning they were to take the train, he couldn't find her. He went to the train station, thinking she was already there, and waited on the platform at the Atocha station for hours. Six trains left for Paris without him, and she never showed up.

Two days later, he was on a plane back to the States. When he arrived home in Chicago, he found a letter waiting that began, *Je suis vraiment désolé...*

I am very sorry...

Ever since, they occasionally ran into each other, usually in Europe, and had a fling for a couple of days. He never got over the fact that she left him at the train station in Madrid. She apologized, but she never gave a satisfactory explanation. Her vagueness angered him. On various occasions, she tried to lure him back into her life.

"Come to Paris now," she would say. "I'm ready."

A couple months later, she would text, "I'll come live with you in DC, but only if you want me to." He never replied to those messages.

He couldn't forgive her, and regardless, he couldn't fathom the idea of being tied down to one woman, so he slept with her once or twice a year like all the other women in his life. Though if he were honest with himself, he would admit that she was always a bit more special than the others. The last time he saw her, he was in Geneva for the World Economic Forum. She became an analyst for the OECD and was there to cover for her organization. He ended their relationship on his way out of the hotel room that final morning. As she lay sleeping, he left her a note that read, *I can't do this anymore...*

That was three years ago.

His heart rate quickened, as he approached the table.

"Bonne nuit, ma bichette," he said.

Lauren turned her gaze toward him and smiled. She got up, and they exchanged kisses on both cheeks. Miles put his hand on the small of her back and pressed himself against her. She pushed her body against his, grabbing and squeezing his bicep, holding that position for a few seconds, like lovers with unfinished business.

"Thank you for coming, Miles."

He saw she was nervous. "How could I refuse a dinner invitation here?"

Lauren smiled. "That's why I chose it."

"You know me well."

"I do."

The waiter arrived, as Miles sat down. He didn't need to study the drink menu, because he knew exactly what he wanted; a 2000 Bordeaux, Smith Haute Laffite.

"A very nice choice, *Monsieur.*"

"And we'll do the tasting menu." He looked at Lauren, who nodded.

"The five, six, or seven course, *Monsieur?*"

"I think the five is plenty," Lauren said.

"The five it is," Miles agreed.

"Bien entendu, Monsieur, Mademoiselle."

The waiter ignored the palpable awkwardness between the two guests. Miles finished removing his coat and checked his phone instinctively before placing it in his pocket. Lauren took a final sip of the wine left in her glass and looked out the window.

"So, how long has it been?" he asked, sipping water and knowing the answer, but curious to see what she would say.

"Geneva, three years ago." She finished the last of her wine. "You left a note."

"Mmmm."

"Mmmm, indeed." Lauren, raising her eyebrows, stared

out the window again.

"I came, didn't I?" He didn't know why he was getting defensive. She always had the uncanny ability to unnerve him more than anyone else.

"You did, and I thanked you."

"So, what did you want to talk about?"

Before she could answer, the waiter returned with the bottle of Bordeaux. He made a show of presenting it to Miles, who nodded. The waiter opened the wine and poured a sip into a glass. Miles swirled the liquid and looked at the color against the backdrop of the white linen on the table. His nose twitched. Lauren rolled her eyes, knowing what was coming, as Miles buried his nose into the glass and inhaled deeply.

"Hmmm. I can tell it's turned already." He took a small sip to confirm it was bad. "Yes. It's not good. Please being another one."

"Are you sure, *Monsieur*?" the waiter asked, a tinge of annoyance in his voice.

"Of course, I'm sure. I ordered it. I was at the vineyard the year they bottled that vintage. I've had several bottles of this wine. I have the vintner's phone number. Should I call her?"

"I'm sorry, *Monsieur*. I'll bring you another bottle."

"You had to do that, didn't you?" Lauren asked, as the waiter walked sheepishly away.

"What? The wine really *had* turned. I'm not going to pay 200 euros to drink a bad bottle of wine. Besides, he was acting like a prick."

"I suppose." She sighed and adjusted the watch on her wrist.

"So...?"

She became visibly nervous, leaning forward to speak to him, her voice low. "Miles, you remember Yemen?"

He frowned in surprise. "Of course, I remember Yemen." He could still smell the stale cigarettes and asbestos in the hotel lobby. He remembered the nauseous, empty pit in his gut when talking with John Carpenter from the CIA about what had happened only a few blocks away.

"Well, I was recently in Beirut, having drinks with some friends and others I did not know," Lauren said. Her French accent grew stronger when she drank. She pulled a cigarette from her purse and lit it, then offered one to Miles, who shook his head. "One of those was an investigative journalist, and he told a story he was working on about the attempted kidnapping and assassination of Sheikh Mohammed Abdullah in Sana'a a few years back."

Miles sat up straight. The man near them shifted in his chair.

"And?" Miles asked.

"He said he had evidence that the CIA orchestrated the attack and kidnapping, but that it got out of hand. With all the shooting, everyone died. He made contact with a defector from the Sheikh's security team who said he provided an American with the schedule and route the Sheikh intended to take that day. I remembered the conversation we had in Geneva about how you were in Sana'a that same day to meet the Sheikh, but your schedule changed at the last minute. You never told me why you changed your schedule that day."

"No, I didn't." He had trouble believing what she was saying, though his mind raced furiously.

"I don't know." She took a drag and dumped ashes into the ashtray. "I just thought you should know. He's still putting the story together, but he said he'd be ready to publish in a couple of weeks. I thought you might want to read it when it comes out."

"What's the journalist's name?"

"Khaled Hussaini. He works for *Al Akhbar.*"

The waiter returned with another bottle of wine, and they went through the routine again. Miles was so distracted, however, that the waiter could have offered him a bottle of cheap vinegar, and he would have said it was fine. The waiter poured two glasses for them.

They sat for a few moments, not speaking.

"What are you thinking about?" she asked.

"Nothing." He knew he had to go to Beirut and meet Khaled Hussaini.

Lauren knew better than to press him when he looked pensive, so she let it drop. The couple beside them signaled the waiter to bring their check.

"I also wanted to see you again," Lauren said, softer than she intended.

Miles, not hearing her, rapidly typed something into his phone.

"Miles? Did you hear what I said?"

"Huh? No, sorry. One second." He brought up the Kayak app and searched flights to Beirut the following day. A Turkish Airlines flight connecting through Istanbul was leaving in the morning. He booked a one-way business-class ticket and put his phone back into his pocket.

"What did you say?" he asked.

"You won't ever change, will you?"

"What do you mean?"

"Nothing. I'm so stupid." Lauren gulped the last of the wine in her glass and began gathering her things. "I'm leaving."

"Lauren, come on. The first course hasn't even arrived. Where are you going?"

She got up and rushed toward the exit. Miles tried to hold onto her arm, but she pulled free. She almost bowled over the waiter, who was bringing the first course.

"We'll be right back," Miles told the man, following her outside.

"Lauren, stop!"

She whirled, tears streaming down her face. Miles stopped

53

a few feet from her. She looked the same she had all those years earlier, the night they were caught in the rain in Madrid and wandered the streets until the breakfast bars opened so they could eat *churros con chocolate.* That was the night they fell in love. They'd been just kids back then.

"What's the matter?" He searched her face for clues.

"The matter is that I still love you."

"Ah." He looked down and ran his hand through his hair. "We've been through this before, Lauren. I thought we had…an understanding." He trained his heart over the years to harden itself toward her, but he felt something breaking. He balled his right hand into a fist and stared down at the ground, shaking his head.

"I know we did, Miles. You and your rules, but my heart doesn't follow those rules. I'm sorry. I'm sorry about Madrid. I know you still don't forgive me for that, even after all these years. I messed up the first time, and you won't forgive me. You never will." She pulled out a cigarette and lit it. The wind increased, and the air felt colder.

"Come back inside," he said. "Let's finish dinner."

"I can't. I did what I came here for. I thought it was important that you know about Khaled, and I hoped, like a stupid woman, to see in your eyes if there was any love in there left for me, but I can see there is not."

Miles couldn't muster the strength to look up at her, and he didn't speak. She stared at him, silently pleading with him to look up at her. She still held out a final, desperate hope that Miles would pull her off the ledge where she stood.

He kept his eyes fixed to the ground. She finally acknowledged that it was over, so she jumped.

"Good–bye, Miles." She turned and walked away, tears coming strongly.

Miles watched her walk away without trying to stop her. He felt that was the last time he would ever see her. Even after all these years, the emotions between them were incredibly strong, and he almost cracked.

Stupid heart, he told himself. *What the fuck do you think you're doing?*

He turned and walked back into the restaurant.

CHAPTER EIGHT

Taxi drivers are the best people to talk to in any city in the world. There's no better plugged-in group of people. They spend all day driving other people around their city, having conversations, sitting in traffic, feeling the mood and understanding the pulse better than anyone else. Always ask your cabbie two questions: What's the current mood in your city or country, and what's the best place to get a beer with the locals?

The driver was having trouble finding the offices of *Al Akhbar*. Miles tried the paper's number again, but no one answered. He tried Khaled's cell number several times from his hotel room the previous night before landing in Beirut, but the phone rang endlessly.

The sun was hot and bright without a cloud in the sky, and the pale, white sides of the buildings intensified the reflection. Miles had to squint even through his sunglasses. He studied the buildings they passed, trying to identify what street and block they were on.

The driver pulled up to a group of men standing on the corner and asked them the paper's office location in Arabic. All four men simultaneously began talking and pointing down the street. From their accents, Miles identified them as Palestinian. A few minutes later, the cab arrived in front of what looked like an apartment building.

"They said this was it," the driver told him in Arabic.

Miles squinted out the window to look. *Fuck it. I'll just get out.* "*Shukran,* thank you," he said, paying the man enough to cover the fare and a tip.

It was the correct building. He found the *Al Akhbar* offices on the third floor, surprised at how small the newsroom was for being the country's fifth-most-read newspaper. Independent and progressive, *Al Akhbar* made waves a few years earlier as one of the first outlets to publish the State Department cables leaked by Wikileaks. There must have been a dozen or more staff, most staring at their computer screens. Inaudible phone conversations intermingled with the constant humming of a copying machine, while the smell of freshly printed newspapers permeated the air. The latest copy sat in a pile in the reception area.

Miles walked up to the front desk and inquired about Khaled. The young woman behind the counter picked up the phone and dialed a number. She hung up a few seconds later.

"Doesn't look like he's in the office today," she said.

"Can you give him this when he comes in?" He handed her a handwritten note with his name and hotel information on it. "Tell him it's about Yemen."

***

Miles was in the hotel bathroom when his phone rang. Wiping his hands on a towel, he walked across the room to the phone by the window. "Hello?"

"Hello. Is this Mr. Miles Davis?" It was a native Arabic speaker with a thick accent, and the line quality was poor.

Miles closed the window to block the street noise. "Yes. Khaled?"

"No, this isn't Khaled." The man paused. "My name is Bilal Abdullah, his colleague at *Al Akhbar.* Well, former colleague. Khaled is dead."

Miles couldn't move for a second.

"The police found him in apartment this evening. One shot to head. We worry when he not show for work today. He never miss day before. Our receptionist say you come look for him this morning and leave note. Can we meet, talk in person?"

Miles hung up and stared at the phone for a moment. *Holy. Fucking. Shit.*

He walked to the bed, sat down, and rubbed his hand through his hair. Thoughts bounced through his mind like unwieldy atoms, making as much sense as quantum physics: Yemen; John on the park bench in DC; the rain in Bogota; Lauren; lunch that day.

He was startled out of his temporary stupor when the phone rang again a few seconds later. "Hello?" he asked dumbly.

"Mr. Miles, it is Bilal. The phone cut. Please, let us meet if you can."

Miles hesitated, wondering if he was in danger. *For what?* he wondered. *It's silly to think I'm in danger.*

Still, the man he flew all that way to see was cold and dead in a morgue with a bullet hole in his head.

"Sure," he said finally.

"OK. Meet me at Al Falamanki. I'll be there in twenty minutes."

***

The traffic was tight but not crushing at that time of night. Miles stared blankly out the taxi window, as it snaked up Damascus Road. Al Falamanki Café sat near St. Joseph's University in the heart of downtown Beirut. A casual place, it was frequented by expats, tourists, and locals. Miles finally felt at ease when he saw it was crowded.

I doubt I'll be shot with this many people around.

Bilal said on the phone he would be wearing a white suit. Miles scanned the crowd and saw someone who fit that description, sitting on a sofa couch in the middle of the garden. Several people were scattered around, smoking *shisha,* drinking, and eating.

He walked up to the man. "Bilal?"

"Yes. Mr. Miles?"

"Yes."

Bilal stood and shook Miles' hand. They stared deeply into each other's eyes. Miles saw dark-brown circles that spoke volumes about the things that man had witnessed in his life. Ghosts were trapped in there. Bilal saw blue eyes holding weariness, underlined by fear.

"Thank you for coming to meet me, Mr. Miles. I apologize for my English."

"*Yumkinuna an natakalam al-arabiya, idha turid,'*" Miles said, surprised that his Arabic wasn't rusty. "We can speak Arabic if you want."

Bilal's eyes bulged in surprise, though he was immediately thankful he wouldn't have to suffer through the conversation in English.

"Oh. Very well, then!" He smiled and replied in his native tongue. "What a relief! I used to speak English when I was younger, but I was never able to fully get the language. Very strange structure, the English language. Where did you learn your Arabic, Mr. Miles?"

"Here and there." He recalled his time in Amman fifteen years earlier. It was one of his first international gigs, advising the king of Jordan, Abdullah II, who had just ascended to the throne. Miles and the king were friends at Georgetown in the '80s, where they ran around together on weekends chasing girls. When he ascended the throne, the king asked Miles to stay in Amman for a while as his unofficial advisor, someone he trusted completely, someone with whom he could have open, candid conversations about how to run his country.

Miles spent eighteen months in Amman, traveling with the king on his first few international trips. That's how Miles got his foot in the door in international politics and where he perfected his Arabic. He met dozens of heads of state. More importantly, he met the people behind the curtains. When he got back to DC, he opened Verge Consulting.

"Very well, then." Bilal flagged a waiter and ordered a hookah pipe with rose tobacco. "What did you want to see Khaled about?"

Miles looked around suspiciously before leaning closer. "I recently had dinner with a friend in Brussels. She told me she met Khaled here in Beirut a few weeks ago, and he was talking about an investigative report he was doing on the attempted CIA kidnapping of Sheikh Mohammed Abdullah in Yemen that ended in a bloody street battle a couple years ago."

"Ah, yes." Bilal inhaled smoke from the pipe.

"I was in Sana'a that day and was supposed to meet the Sheikh," Miles said, wondering how much he should say.

"What were you meeting him for?"

"He was looking to diversify his portfolio in Central America. I know a few key players in that region. I was going to start making connections for him there."

"What do you do, Mr. Miles?"

"I run a political consultancy firm in Washington, DC."

"Interesting." He offered the hookah hose to Miles, who took it, replaced the mouthpiece with a fresh tip, and inhaled deeply. Smooth, cool smoke filled his lungs, and the sweet taste of rose danced on his tongue. He was still weighing just how much he could trust this man. His mind was in survival mode. He blew the smoke slowly out of his nose.

"Did you meet with the Sheikh?"

"I was about to go to the meeting when a man in the lobby stopped me and advised against it."

"Who was this man?"

Miles shifted in his seat and handed the hose back to Bilal, immediately regretting he mentioned that specific detail. "I don't remember."

Bilal smiled, knowing Miles was lying. He inhaled from the hose and returned it to Miles. "There's something you aren't telling me, Mr. Miles."

"I don't know how much I can trust you."

"Fair enough, but you came all this way to meet a man who is now dead, and I'm the only one who knows what he knew. Tell me who the man was you talked to at the hotel."

Miles looked around, fearing to say out loud it was John, the CIA agent, because it could seriously jeopardize his own safety. Instead, he asked, "So you know what Khaled was writing about?"

"Of course, I do. I have all his notes and an almost-finished version of his story." He inhaled from the pipe. "A few weeks ago, Khaled grew suspicious and nervous about what he was uncovering. He gave me a password to an email account and said if anything happened to him, I should access that email."

"What did he write?"

"What your friend told you. He wrote, and has proof, that the CIA was responsible for the kidnapping attempt."

"Do you think he was murdered for what he was writing?"

"You tell me, Mr. Miles."

Miles sat back in his chair and removed his glasses, rubbing the bridge of his nose with his thumb and forefinger. He cleaned the lenses with the bottom of his shirt.

"Nothing was stolen from his apartment," Bilal said. "There were no signs of a break-in. He was shot in the back of the head. The police found him face down a few feet from his front door. It appeared he opened the door and turned around to walk inside. Whoever was at the door shot him, closed the door, and left."

"So, whoever it was, Khaled knew him?"

"It appears so."

Miles shook his head, not wanting to believe the way the pieces were falling into place. Had they set up the kidnapping in Yemen and warned him just to place Miles in their debt? A nagging doubt about the whole situation floated in the murky backwaters of his consciousness, but he was afraid to bring it front and center to confront it. Suddenly, it was thrust upon him.

"Do the police have any leads?" Miles asked.

"No. It was a professional job, very clean, no evidence. It doesn't matter. Khaled was finished with the article, something his assailants don't know. I'm only finalizing the edits now. The article will be published next week."

Bilal called the waiter over to order food. "Do you want anything?" he asked Miles.

Miles shook his head.

"If something happens to me before publication, I set a dead man's switch that will email the article to several journalists around the world."

Very smart, Miles thought. The automatic trigger would distribute the information if the account holder didn't log in every seventy-two hours.

"The story will come out one way or another. It would be nice if we could have it corroborated by you, if you have any information you can give me."

Miles again ignored the request. "Thank you for letting me know. I look forward to reading it when it comes out."

"You're leaving so soon?"

"Yes. Sorry. I have to get back to Washington." Miles stood, and Bilal stood, too. Staring at each other, they shook hands.

Bilal handed Miles a card. "My contact information, Mr. Miles, in case you remember anything."

"Yeah, sure."

Bilal watched Miles leave the patio. He flagged a taxi and gave the driver the name of his hotel.

***

Once back in his room, Miles threw his belongings into his suitcase, went downstairs, and checked out. He took a taxi straight to the airport, where he bought a one-way ticket to Dulles, connecting through Frankfurt. His plane would leave in three hours.

After going through security, he walked to the business lounge. He ordered a double shot whisky, neat, and sat in a lounge chair overlooking the runway, watching planes take off and land until it was time for his flight.

CHAPTER NINE

David: Hey, just landed.
Lisa: Great! At hotel already. You hungry?
David: Yeah. Starving.
Lisa: Me 2. I'll wait for you to get dinner?
David: Sounds good. Will txt you when ready.
Lisa: Prem exec lounge?
David: Anywhere else? ;)
Lisa: LOL. Of course not. See you soon. :)

David walked through the elevator doors on the executive lounge floor and approached the desk attendant.

"Welcome, Mr. Strasbourg," the attendant said, having been briefed at the start of her shift with photographs of the VIPs staying with them. She spent the first ten minutes of her shift memorizing them with her colleague, flash-card style. "You have access to our premier executive lounge. Please take the staircase up to the top if you wish."

"Thanks," David said, and headed up the stairs.

The hotel's premier executive lounge above the normal executive lounge was accessible to only two types of people: celebrities and guests who spent over $50k a year at their facilities worldwide. David, Miles, and Lisa fell into the latter category, easily hitting that mark each year.

David opened the door at the top of the staircase with his room key and scanned the space for Lisa. She was on the veranda at a corner bar table, a glass of red wine and an assortment of olives, cheeses, and crackers before her. Bogota at night that time of year was chilly, so she wore a navy-blue suit skirt and a white button-up blouse topped by a bright pink and purple pashmina scarf. He recognized it as the one they bought together in Mumbai.

They embraced warmly, David seeing by her eyes that she wasn't on her first glass of wine. She smelled of lavender.

"Good flight?" she asked.

"Not bad. I like these short assignments to Latin America."

"Right?! It's those Asian flights that always get me."

"Yup. I see you started the evening already."

"You know it." She gave him a coy smile and waved to the waiter behind the bar. "I assume you're having your usual?"

"Yes, please."

When the bartender approached, Lisa spoke in perfect Spanish, "Ardbeg, neat, for the *Señor.*"

"With pleasure," the bartender said.

"You know me too well."

Lisa smiled and sipped her wine. The falling sun finally moved past the hazy horizon, and the coming night set out its customary accoutrements. Small globes of light dotted the city's darkened canvas. Wafts of greasy food floated up from the street below. Even the car horns had a unique sound at that time of day. Faint cumbia music joined the assortment from a nearby apartment.

David kept his suit coat on and sat across from Lisa. A light breeze brushed their cheeks. Glancing out across the city, he took a deep breath to inhale it all in.

There's nothing like the first night in a new place.

"Miles make it?" David asked.

"Yes. He's having dinner with Alfredo and Henry."

"Great."

"We're meeting Monday morning at ten."

"Very good. Man, I'm hungry." He grabbed one of her olives.

"Let's order. Waiter!"

He came to take their order. They looked out again over the city, enjoying the Bogota skyline as one in a long string of cities where they had shared a meal and a drink—Istanbul, Mumbai, Berlin—and that was just in the last six months.

As was their custom, which Miles had taught them, they arrived on a Saturday before the work week to take advantage of having Sunday to rest and recuperate from jet lag. They could have easily arrived on Sunday for that trip, because Bogota was only a few hours from DC by plane, but force of habit made them both book tickets to leave and arrive on Saturday. They hadn't even checked with each other. Both assumed the normal plan was in place for the project.

Something was different about that night, though. Lisa seemed more on edge, David sensed. He knew her well enough to know she wanted to talk about something but was holding back. He recalled their conversation at ChurchKey a few weeks earlier.

"Just ask me," he said.

"Huh?" Caught off guard, she took her napkin from her lap and dabbed her lip.

"What is it? You've been acting weird since I got here."

"What are you talking about? I'm not acting weird." She shifted in her eat.

"OK." He regretted his statement, because it increased the tension between them.

"It's just...nothing."

"Go on."

She bit her lip and looked toward the bar for the bartender.

"Tell you what," David said, desperate to ease the awkwardness. "It's Saturday night, and we don't have to

66

work tomorrow. After we eat, let's go dancing. What do you say?"

Lisa, startled and excited by the proposition, wiped her mouth and considered the idea.

"Come on. It'll be fun! I checked online today for places we could go near the hotel, and there's a salsa bar just a couple blocks from here. We can walk."

"So, you've been planning this?"

David blushed and smiled. Lisa laughed and reached across the table to touch his arm. He tensed slightly.

"Yeah," she said. "Let's do it."

***

Salsa Camara sits on Calle 71 in northern Bogota. A small, dingy club with low ceilings and dark lighting, it more than made up for the sparse décor with fantastic live music and cheap drinks.

David left his sport coat at the hotel. Lisa changed into a free-flowing dress. They laughed and talked all the way to the bar. When they arrived, they found it packed. Well-dressed Colombians and expats filled the place, dancing and twirling on the small floor.

David grabbed Lisa's hand to avoid losing her in the throng and headed to the bar. He waved the bartender down and mouthed, "*Dos margaritas.*"

The bartender nodded. They clinked glasses when the man handed them their drinks and looked at each other with devilish grins.

The band ramped up with a fast, jazz-infused, free-flow salsa, feeding off the heat and energy emanating from the crowd. There were some excellent salsa dancers on the floor. Three couples in particular showed off moves they'd been practicing and perfecting since they were little kids running around adult's legs at weddings.

Lisa tossed her head back to finish her drink and gave David a one eyebrow raised, sarcastic, and impatient look.

"What?" he asked, sipping from his straw and doing a poor job trying to hide behind his cup.

"I thought you brought me here to dance." She placed one hand on her hip.

"All right, all right!" He tossed back his own drink, grabbed her hand, and nudged their way to an open spot on the dance floor. Both knew the basic steps, but Lisa was a more-experienced dancer. They danced closer as each song blended into the next, getting lost in the swell of sweaty, salty revelers, all of them forgetting the outside world for the moment.

David's hands pulled on her hips, and she pressed her chest against his. He would then lead her to spin away from him, silently counting the steps he needed to take, desperately trying to keep up with the music and the other dancers. Lisa's easy flow and playful demeanor did a good job of covering up his mistakes. Their noses touched a few times, but neither was brave enough to make the first move.

A handsome Colombian man in a tight, black shirt asked David if he could dance with his wife. Not wanting to get into a conversation about their marital status in a crowded dance floor, he simply said, "Yes, of course." He and Lisa wore rings on their left hands, so it was easy to understand why the man mistook them for a married couple.

The man took Lisa's hand and began twirling her. She followed his direction perfectly. The temperature in the club seemed to keep rising, and everyone was soaked in sweat. The rhythm of the music inexorably shook hips and moved feet.

Lisa's face perspired, and her curls started to frizz, but she looked gorgeous and exotic. Her red hair and white porcelain skin stood in sharp contrast to the darker haired Colombians. Smiling and laughing, she spun, completely in control yet also totally free. It looked like she'd been dancing salsa her entire life.

After the dance, the Colombian kissed her hand and thanked David for allowing the privilege. David raised his cup, as Lisa came back to give him a huge hug.

"You were incredible!" David shouted over the music.

Slightly out of breath, she nodded. "Yeah! He was great. I just followed what he told me to do. I never spun so much before!"

David laughed. "It was something to watch. Let's get another drink."

"Sure!" Lisa smiled and looked back over the crowded dance floor.

They stayed and danced until the lights came on and the bar staff was forced to ask people to leave. Dawn's light was washing away the stars when they stepped outside.

"Let's nightcap in my room," David suggested. "I have a bottle of wine we can pop open."

Lisa regarded him. "You sure that's a good idea?"

"Yeah. Why not? The night was way too much fun to end now. We can have one more drink before we call it an evening."

"OK." Lisa said.

***

Entering his room, Lisa shot straight for the bathroom while David went to the wet bar and pulled out the bottle of Pinot Noir from the small fridge. He took two stemless wine glasses from the overhead cabinet and fumbled for the cork key in the drawer until he realized it was a screw top cap. After skimming through Spotify on his phone, he put on Hozier, and the opening notes of *Cherry Wine* softly filled the room.

Lisa came out of the bathroom and walked to the couch facing the window and the Bogota skyline. *No matter how different cities around the world are,* she thought, *they're all peaceful at dawn.* She remembered the muezzin call to prayer in the Muslim countries she'd visited. *If I were there, I'd be hearing them now.*

David walked over with the wineglasses and set them on the coffee table. They considered each other for a minute before David spoke.

"Come on, Lish. Talk to me. You didn't tell me what's up at dinner. What's on your mind?"

He never called me that before. It was her childhood nickname that only her parents and brother used. It was her comfort name, used in her comfort space, where he just intruded, yet it felt strangely comfortable.

She took a big sip from her wine glass. "It's Stewart. We had a big fight before I took off, and I left angry."

"I'm sorry to hear that."

"Yeah. What can you do?"

"Are you rethinking the marriage?"

Lisa, sipping from her glass again, stared out the window. She'd thought of it, of course, but she always pushed the thought away. She felt her nagging mother's presence sitting in the back of her conscience, reminding her that she burned down the house of every potential partner she'd ever had. She didn't want to burn this house down. She loved Stewart.

"I mean, I love him. He's a great guy—funny and smart— and he treats me really well."

"So, what's the problem?"

"I don't know." She glanced back and saw David staring at her. He was drunk. So was she. Silence hung between them.

"David, do you ever think of me...like that?"

"Like what?"

"You know. Like more than just the colleague who's smarter than you?"

"Hey now!" He playfully hit her arm and let his hand rest

closer to her thigh. She gave a half-laugh, half-snort that embarrassed her. They both laughed out loud.

"I'm married, Lisa."

"I know, and I'm engaged."

"So, what does it matter if I ever think of you like that?"

"I don't know. Curiosity getting the better of me, I guess."

Another silence hung in the air, yet this one was charged with unmistakeable sexual tension. A thousand thoughts raced through each of their minds. Lisa crossed her legs, exposing more of her thigh. Eye contact became awkward. David, pursing his lips, put his hand on her leg.

"Yes."

"Yes, what?"

"The answer to your question is, yes." He leaned over and kissed her.

Passion boiled over, and they kissed deeply, beginning to remove each other's clothes. He leaned back, and she straddled him from the top. His hands slid underneath her dress and moved up her thighs to her waist.

She put her hands on his chest and pushed away. "David, we can't do this."

"Yes, we can. Come on. I thought this was what you wanted."

"It is, but it's not. It's complicated. We'll both regret it. I'm sorry. I shouldn't have brought it up or come to your room."

She got off him and buttoned the front of her dress. David sat, confused by the wild swings of emotion.

"Fine." Anger, confusion, and sexual frustration swirled in him. *Was it something I said or did?* "I won't insist."

"I'll see you in the morning, OK?" She said, her back towards him.

"Yeah." He got up and walked toward the window. "See you in the morning."

She opened the door and left. David stood for a moment, trying to process what just happened. A few minutes later and he still hadn't moved. Neither the increasingly clear skyline outside nor the waking city below offered answers.

His phone vibrated with an incoming text message. He picked it up.

Lisa: I'm sorry again. :(

David: Don't be. I'm frankly surprised it hadn't happened sooner.

David: I liked it.

Lisa: Really? You aren't mad?

David: No.

He set the phone back down and rubbed his hand through his hair, scratching the back of his neck and yawning. The night had exhausted him, physically as well as mentally and emotionally. A few seconds later, his phone buzzed again.

Lisa: Do you want to come to my room?

David: Yes.

Lisa: 586.

He grabbed his phone charger from the side of the bed and his toothbrush from the bathroom, then stepped out of his room.

Chapter Ten

The alarm was a cruel beckoning to start the day. David opened one eye and picked up his phone from the side table. It was 7:28 AM. He gently pressed his thumb on the home button of his i-Phone and went to his email.

How many times have I done this exact motion first thing in the morning?

He had twenty-eight unread emails. Twenty were from Miles.

"Miles has been up for a while," a voice said beside him.

He rolled over and saw Lisa lying on her side, exposed from the waist up, looking at him. He smiled and kissed her.

"Hi."

"Hi."

He put his arms around her and pulled, kissing her long and deep. He felt himself getting aroused, as did Lisa.

"No, no, no," she said, pushing his chest. "We gotta get ready. Miles will be waiting in the breakfast room."

"C'mon. A quick one before we start the day."

They made love for the first time two nights earlier, after Lisa texted David to come to her room. They spent all day Sunday in the hotel, going at it multiple times. They ordered room service for breakfast, lunch, and dinner, not bothering one bit to do any sight-seeing.

"No!" She giggled, hitting him with her pillow. She jumped out of bed, covered herself with a bed sheet, and

73

went to the bathroom.

Smiling to himself, he grabbed his phone again and began reading his email.

"It's Monday," she called from the bathroom. "We have to be ready to work. Plus, we did it at least four times in the last forty-eight hours. Aren't you satiated?"

"I don't think I'll ever be satiated with you."

"Ha! Are you gonna shower here or in your room?"

David heard she was in the middle of brushing her teeth. "I guess I'll head up."

"That's probably a good idea." She popped her head around the corner. "See you downstairs?"

David got up, dressed, and went to the bathroom, where he kissed the back of her head. She gave him a coy look in the mirror before spitting in the sink. He smacked her butt and she gave a slight squeal.

***

David, walking through the hotel's restaurant doors, scanned the room. He spotted the others and made his way toward their table. Miles was in his usual suit and open-collared shirt. Lisa was already there, as was Henry Martin. Coffee mugs, half-eaten croissants, and pieces of fruit were on several plates in front of them.

How'd she get ready faster than me? he wondered.

"Morning," he said, approaching the table, purposefully not looking at Lisa.

All three looked up. Henry smiled and stood to give David a big hug. He was a good-looking man in his late forties. With wavy blond hair, blue eyes, and a perpetual dark tan, he looked like a stereotypical California beach bum, though he was originally from Australia and had moved to the United States for college. Like David, Henry started out as a volunteer on a Miles-run campaign, and ever since had worked in one form or another for Miles and with David. He was Verge Consulting's Business Development Director and had been ever since the company was formed. He was constantly on the road, ginning up business for the company. David considered Henry a good friend, and Henry returned the sentiment, though they only ever saw each other in person a handful of times a year.

Curious about where Henry lived, David once asked their Human Resources Director. She said she didn't know, and that she only sent Henry's W-2's each year to a P.O. Box in Helena, Montana.

The only blemish on Henry's clean-shaven face was a thin scar that cut from his left ear to the edge of his chin. David heard at least three stories about how he got that cut—a Turkish prostitute who accused him of short-changing her; a bar fight in Johannesburg after a rugby match; and a rock-climbing accident in Yosemite Valley. Henry would tell one of those stories depending on the situation he found himself in. The truth, however, was much tamer than any of those tall tales—he'd slipped in the shower room in high school and sliced his chin on the towel rail. But only a handful of close friends knew that.

"Davey, great to see you, Mate." Henry said in his strong, Aussie accent.

"Likewise, Henry. I'm glad you made the trip. Where are you coming from?"

"Kenya. I met the Prime Minister. We might have an in there."

"Excellent." David smiled and looked at Miles, who'd gone back to his newspaper. He glanced at Lisa, who gave him her normal smile, as if the last forty-eight hours hadn't happened.

I need to learn that look, he realized.

"Eat up, Davey-boy," Miles said without looking up, mimicking Henry's accent. "We should head over soon.

They are expecting us within the hour."

***

Enrique Arenas' campaign headquarters were in a nondescript office building near Parque de la 93 in Chico Norte, an upscale neighborhood on the east side of the city. Cafés, restaurants, and little boutique shops ringed the well-kept park, where young couples lounged on the grass, old men paced in pairs with their hands behind their backs, and little old ladies gossiped while taking their dogs for walks.

Miles, David, Henry, and Lisa poured from the cab and walked up the building's steps to take the elevator to the third floor. Alfredo, there to greet them at the door, led them into a conference room full of people and noise.

Enrique was there, and, when he saw the Americans walk in, rose to greet them. The room became noticeably quieter, as the focus shifted to the four newcomers. Alfredo made the introductions, and Enrique warmly shook their hands. They moved around, shaking hands with everyone else, as Enrique introduced them.

David saw all the men checking Lisa out and felt a pang of jealousy. *That's interesting,* he thought.

Miles and his team already knew the others, having received a detailed dossier on Enrique and his people from Alfredo before their trip.

"There are a few of these guys we'll have to keep an eye on," Henry said in the cab on the way over.

"Let me guess," Miles said. "Davidson and Tomas."

"Why do you say that?" Lisa asked.

"Because they're the strategy and research guys," Henry said.

"The guys whose jobs we're taking," David explained, sitting next to Lisa with their legs touching in the cramped back seat of the small cab. He tried very hard to keep his hand away from her lap.

She gave him a quick hard look that said, *Don't you dare,* with her eyes.

His palms began to sweat.

After shaking the last person's hand, Enrique pointed to one side of the table with four empty chairs and motioned for the American team to sit down.

"So," he began, "welcome again to Colombia."

"We're thrilled to be here *Señor* Arenas," Miles replied.

"Please, call me Enrique. My father is *Señor* Arenas."

The room vented in nervous laughter, immediately releasing the tension that built up over their arrival and the awkward introductions. The rest of the afternoon, they discussed the various strategic approaches the Verge team had put together. David explained the overall strategy, with Lisa jumping in to highlight particular points. Miles let his two protégés do most of the talking.

After each point or a brief break in the conversation, everyone looked to Enrique to gauge his reaction. Most of them were positive. He asked insightful questions, to which the team had prepared thoughtful responses. The Colombian team also asked questions, at first with thinly veiled condescension, but, as the meeting stretched out, they realized the *gringos* knew what they were talking about, so their respect grew. David and Lisa gave Miles a quick glance at times, always receiving his approval with a slight nod. They were killing it in that meeting, and all three knew it.

When the presentation ended, Enrique gave big hugs all around. Everyone was in a cheerful, positive mood. The campaign had infrastructure and a solid plan for victory. Enrique called for whisky, and a nondescript maid materialized with a bottle of Ardbeg and some eight-ball glasses.

"Freddy tells me you're a single-malt man," Enrique said to David.

"He said you were the same," David replied. "That's why we took the job."

The others laughed and toasted.

"There are still one or two points I need to think about for the platform," Enrique said.

David glanced at Miles, who was wearing his poker face. David knew that face—the slight tightening of the lips at the corners belied his surprise and anger.

"I'll discuss it with my team here, and we'll be in touch."

"We're part of the campaign now, Enrique," Miles said.

"Of course, you are, *Señor* Miles, but there are a few internal things we need to discuss. We will of course keep you in the loop."

Miles didn't like the disingenuous smile on Enrique's face.

"All in due time, Miles," Freddy said walking over and patting him on the back. He tried to stem the rising tension in the room. "Don't worry. To the campaign!"

"To Colombia," Enrique said.

"To Colombia!"

***

The plane banked hard on its ascent from El Dorado International Airport, leaving a cloudy Bogota behind. After a brief announcement from the captain, detailing their altitude and flight time to Dulles International Airport, the plane steadied, and the airline stewardesses began the beverage service.

David put his hand on Lisa's knee, and she placed her hand on top of his.

"So, what do we do from here?" he asked.

"Nothing. We do nothing."

"We pretend the last few days didn't happen?"

"What do you suggest, David?" A mixture of slight anger and regret tinged her words. She re-crossed her legs to force

David's hand off.

"Would you like a drink, *Señor?*" The stewardess set a napkin on David's fold-out table and another on Lisa's.

"Yes. Scotch, neat, please."

"And for you *Señorita?*"

"A glass of red wine, please."

The stewardess walked back to the galley and brought back their orders, setting two peanut bags beside each glass. David glanced out the window to see if he could see city lights, but the clouds went all the way to the horizon.

"I guess you're right," he said finally.

"I mean, you're married, David, with a little boy and another on the way. And I'm engaged to Stewart. What else can we do?"

"No. You're right. There's nothing we can do."

They sat together, but each was lost in their own thoughts. David finished his drink quickly and flagged down the stewardess for another. Lisa unlocked her phone and scrolled for something in her notes.

"I wrote this last night." She set the phone on his table.

He saw it was a poem.

Darling be careful, it's bright,
This diamond, this light,
A treasure to hold?
Or an addiction too bold?
Can it truly be, for you and me?
I was starving from within,
Lost in false hope, where to begin,
Ignore the smoke,
It's normal to choke,
My heart says with glee.
Yet now there you stand,
Me blooming in your hand,
Be gentle please,

I'm down on my knees,
Not sure how much of this addiction is free.

He read it twice, then said, "Wow."

Lisa took her phone back, embarrassed at having shared the poem with him. She sipped her wine.

"I didn't know you wrote poetry," he said.

"I don't. Well, I used to when I was a girl, but not for a long time. I guess I was, inspired." She smiled coyly.

David smiled back. Taking his phone from the seat pocket, he searched for something on it before setting it on her table.

"I guess I was inspired, too."

You, insatiable you,
A whirlwind firestorm of red and curls,
Of curves and spark,
Please, have a taste
But don't leave a mark.
Subject to circumstance,
Believe me or not,
This ride is more than I bargained for.
Throw it up,
Throw it all up in the air,
Let's see what we can catch
And what falls to shatter on the ground,
I do wonder how that would sound?
A friend once said there's something so wretched about this,
Yet something so precious about this.
Where to begin, indeed.

Lisa smiled and leaned over to kiss him. David held her bottom lip softly in his teeth and dabbed it with his tongue. She pushed forward and sucked gently on his upper lip. Their eyes locked for a few seconds as they continued to make out, a crushing gravitational pull that was felt strongly and equally on both sides.

Leaning back in her chair, she took out her headphones and plugged them into her phone.

"What are we going to do?" David asked rhetorically, relishing the taste of her mouth in his.

"I don't know." Lisa hit *Play* and peered out the window toward the endless horizon as Hozier sounded in her ears. "I don't know."

CHAPTER ELEVEN

"It has to be the centerpiece of my platform," Enrique said. "It's what the people want."

He was annoyed at the amount of pushback he was getting from Miles and David. They were on speakerphone from DC. Alfredo and the rest of Enrique's Colombian team were in the conference room headquarters in Bogota.

"I know, Enrique," Miles said, "but it'll spook the markets and you'll lose political support in the U.S. and Europe." He looked at the clock. It was 11:34 PM in DC, making it 9:34 PM in Colombia.

"I'm running for president of Colombia and for the Colombian people, Miles, not for the *gringos* or the international markets."

"I fully understand that." Miles felt the strain of the three-month-long campaign in general and that day's fourteen-hour workday in particular.

David flipped through piles of focus group transcripts and poll numbers on the opposite side of the conference table. A pen dangled from his mouth, the end mangled from continuous chewing. Enrique was in a closer race than any of them expected. With only a couple weeks left before the election, everyone was nervous.

"But if you nationalize Bancolombia, there will be a massive withdrawal of financial support from your country," Miles continued, "both in the public and private sectors. That will have a devastating effect on your economy."

"Our biggest export is oil. With crude at $97 a barrel, we feel we can weather the initial storm this would cause," Davidson said, "and things would settle down. We're the largest producer of coal in Latin America."

Enrique nodded at him, then said, "Controlling Colombia's largest bank will put us in a strong position to push through the reforms we want."

Miles muted the line for a moment. "Their biggest fucking export is cocaine," he told David. He unmuted the line again. "Yes, Davidson, but oil prices fluctuate. Coal prices fluctuate. Nothing is permanent, especially in the commodities markets. The Saudis just announced they're increasing their supply in the market, because they're under a lot of pressure from Washington. We also have an election coming up, and the President wants gas prices to fall, which they will. Nationalization isn't the answer, Enrique. Look at your neighbor to see how well that's worked out."

They heard incoherent Spanish mumbling on the line. Miles gave David an exasperated, puzzled look. David shrugged.

"David, what did you hear when you were in Cali?" Enrique asked.

Cali, one of Colombia's largest cities and a key economic hub in the country, was also a strategic place on the map for Enrique's campaign. Everyone on the team knew if they won Cali, they could take the southwest and secure the election.

"The proposal tested well in Cali." David looked up from the notes of groups he did the previous week. "There's strong anti–IMF and World Bank sentiment there, and the people feel bringing Bancolombia into the government fold is a good thing."

"But Enrique," Miles said quickly, "this is a classic case of people not knowing what's good for them. You know international banking and finance are complex concepts. The global community is too intertwined for you to do this and not have a negative effect. Your country has enacted some great reforms in the last decade. Your economy is starting to diversify and move away from dependence on natural resource exports. This would be turning back the clock and would hurt everyone in the long run."

There was more chatter in Spanish on the other line. Miles muted the line again. "We should have fucking gone down there for this meeting."

David didn't reply. He'd been to Colombia four times in the last two months. The thought of doing it again gave him a headache, though he knew he'd need to make more trips before the election. He wanted to stay home and help around the house. Their second son was born four weeks earlier, and Stacy had post-partum depression. She constantly complained that David was on the road too much and not doing enough with the kids.

"This is how I make a living to support us," he replied.

"Bullshit, David." She held their infant son in her arms, shaking him gently up and down. He wasn't sleeping well, which meant she wasn't, either. Deep purple bags hung from her eyes and her skin was pale. She looked like a ghost of her former self.

"You're smart and talented," she said. "You could do any other job."

"Goddamn it, Stacy, I don't want another job. I love my job. I've never done anything other than work for Miles my entire life."

"Maybe that's the problem." The baby fussed in her arms, and she leaned over to kiss his small forehead, praying he would fall asleep. David, furious to the point that his fingernails dug into the palms of his hand, didn't answer, knowing that would just lead to a louder shouting match and definitely wake up the baby, as well as the two-year old upstairs.

"Do you love me? Do you love your family? Sometimes, I feel you care more about Miles and your job than us." She was frustrated at how distant and cold he'd become lately. He wasn't the man she married.

"Fucking Christ, Stacy." He would then retire to the back porch to sneak a cigarette and drink whisky until he felt a warm buzz. He never admitted it, but he knew he'd never be able to handle a job that tied him to a desk.

Travel was his greatest pleasure. Without it, he would wither and die. *Fernweh*, as the Germans would say. A longing for far off places. David had that word tattooed on his ankle.

Working for someone other than Miles was a horrific thought as well, but he knew Stacy was unhappy and extremely depressed. He even suspected she might know something about his affair with Lisa, though he couldn't imagine how. The way she looked at him had become distant and reserved, yet he couldn't bring himself to care enough to deal with it.

It was like staring down a long train track and seeing the engine coming at him full speed, but he was without any sense of urgency to get out of the way. The thought he didn't love Stacy anymore scared the shit out of him, so whenever it popped into his head, he immediately dismissed it. He couldn't stomach the thought of what it would mean if he actually sat down to confront the idea.

How can you not love your wife anymore, the mother of your two sons?

He and Stacy never took the time to sit down and discuss their marital problems or seek outside counseling. She was too tired and depressed, worried only about getting through the day, one day at a time. He was too wrapped up in work until weeks passed like hours. He was surprised to come home one day to find that his wife had made a cake for their youngest son's one-month birthday. *How had it already been a month?* He hadn't even bought a present.

These small issues that were cancerous to their relationship remained and began to metastasize. He sometimes felt it was better to just stand on the train tracks, close his eyes, and let the train come.

"OK," Enrique said. "We will think more about it. Thank you, David and Miles. Let's call it a night. I know it's late in DC."

"OK, Enrique," Mile said. "I'll send you a memo with the latest data we have from David's trip to Cali. Lisa gets back from Barranquilla on Thursday, and we'll have fresh insight from there. Have a good night."

Miles hung up and leaned back in his chair. After removing his glasses, he pinched the bridge of his nose between his thumb and forefinger.

"That was painful," David said.

"Yeah. Fucking shit! I'm worried he's getting too much bad advice from Davidson and Tomas. Those guys are idiots."

"But the data doesn't lie, Miles. Nationalization of Bancolombia is playing well in the battlegrounds across the country. What I heard in Cali was pretty definitive. If Enrique goes with his plan, he'll have support for it."

"I know, but sometimes, a true leader has to talk straight to his people, even when it's something they don't want to hear. I thought he was that kind of leader."

"We were hired to win him the election, not run the country."

Miles smiled. "That's something I would say."

"Maybe you're slowing down, getting soft in your old age." David smirked.

"Ha. Maybe. All right. You should go home. I'll stick around a little longer and finish this memo."

"I can stay and help."

"No. Get home to Stacy and the boys."

"All right."

As David gathered his things, Miles asked, "David, everything good?"

David paused, giving him a melancholy smile. Miles rarely inquired about his personal life. Maybe the strain of the campaign and his affair were starting to show.

"Yeah, I'm fine. I'm just tired."

"OK. Once this campaign finishes, you should take the family on a vacation to the beach somewhere. It would be good for you and them."

"That sounds like a good idea. Good night, Miles."

"Good night, David."

CHAPTER TWELVE

You have to be careful where and when you discuss anything important or secret in DC. There are countless stories about a story leaking or important information being disclosed during a conversation that can be overheard. Notorious locations are the Metro and the bars during happy hours. DC people not only spend most of their time working, they also spend most of their time outside work talking about it. It's a sad but true fact about this city, especially if something juicy is going down. You've been warned.

John was almost finished with his meal by the time Miles arrived and sat across from him. "You want some?"

"No, thanks. Not hungry."

"Suit yourself." He put the last piece of steak into his mouth, chewed it a couple times, and rinsed it down with the remaining red wine in his glass.

"There's nothing like the steak they serve here," he said, referring to the Capital Grille Restaurant. A DC establishment for decades, the Capital Grille sits prominently on the corners of 6th and Pennsylvania Ave NW, halfway between the Capitol Building and the White House. They offer $50 steaks and four-digit bottles of wine. Patrons rub shoulders with senators, congressmen, lobbyists, and other members of the DC elite who crave an expensive, but delicious, steak dinner.

"I prefer Ray's Steaks myself," Miles said.

"They do it pretty well over there. Have you had their burgers?"

"Yes, I have."

"Man, I sure do love a good piece of meat." He wiped his mouth, folded his napkin, set it on his plate, then gestured to the waiter.

"I know you like cutting straight to the point," John said, "so here it is. We aren't too fond of your boy's plan to nationalize the bank in Colombia."

"Neither am I."

"What are you going to do about it?"

"There isn't much more I *can* do about it, John." Miles felt his blood pressure rising. "I made what I thought were persuasive arguments against it, but the polling in favor of it is too strong. The people love the idea. He can solidify his victory with that on his platform."

"The reason he thinks that is because your research is telling him it is."

"I'm not sure I understand you." Miles knew exactly what John's point was, but he wanted him to say it.

John smiled. "Look, we think Enrique is a fine candidate and could actually be a decent president, but this nationalization idea would be a disaster. Several major American banks stand to lose a lot of money if he goes through with it."

"That isn't my concern. I'm not sure why it's yours, either."

"What's good for American banks is good for America."

"Don't patronize me, you son of a bitch."

"Whoa! Easy there, Miles. No need to get so worked up about it."

"How can I not get worked up over what you're asking me to do?" Miles forced himself to lower his voice and lean over the table. "I won't lie or manipulate my research results to guide my client's policies to your liking. I don't make or create the policies. I only give a clear picture of the political landscape. What my clients do with the information is their business."

"Come on, Miles. You know you have undue influence on your candidates and what they do or don't do."

"Is that what you really think? Man, you guys are dumber than I thought."

"We know he listens to you and to your colleague, David. You built this platform for him, and he accepted all of it. His nationalization plan is pure populism. Not good for anyone."

"You're giving us way too much credit." Miles tried to hide his shock at how much John knew.

"Look, Miles, all we're saying is that he can't go forward with his plan to nationalize Bancolombia."

"Or what?"

The waiter came over with the bill. Miles leaned back, took a deep breath, and studied the bar. The place was crowded for a Thursday night.

John gave the waiter his credit card, and the man left to process the bill. "Why'd you go to Beirut, Miles?"

Miles wasn't surprised John knew about his trip, though it was still unnerving. He didn't answer.

"Did it have anything to do with that ridiculous story in *Al Akbhar* about the Yemeni incident?"

"Yes, actually. A friend told me the article was being written, and I wanted to speak to the author. A funny thing happened, though. He was shot the day I arrived."

"An unfortunate tragedy."

"I'm sure you're heartbroken over it." Miles became angry again. "It didn't matter. The article was published, anyway."

"Yes, and we've vehemently denied any involvement in it. It was just a hit piece by a third-rate conspiratorial-spewing rag trying to sell papers. Conspiracy theories are a dime a dozen in that part of the world."

"The article makes a pretty convincing case. For me, certain unsettling pieces have fallen into place."

"What are you trying to say?" John looked at him hard.

Miles looked out the window, and the waiter returned with John's credit card. He signed the bill and placed it in the presenter.

John stood and grabbed his coat. After taking a few steps, he turned. "Miles, about Bancolombia. Please see to it that Enrique's plan doesn't move forward. Clear?"

"Fuck you, John."

"See you around, Miles." John smiled and left the restaurant.

Miles numbly stumbled to the bar and ordered a double shot of whisky, neat. He sat there shaking his head and thinking. The pieces fit and made sense in an incredibly devious and nefarious way. He just couldn't believe the picture they formed.

After taking a large sip of his drink, he slammed his hand against the bar.

CHAPTER THIRTEEN

All warfare is based on deception. Hence, when we are able to attack, we must seem unable; when using our forces, we must appear inactive; when we are near, we must make the enemy believe we are far away; when far away, we must make him believe we are near.

Sun Tzu
The Art of War

"You can go in now, Mr. Davis. The senator will see you."

Miles set the copy of *Politico* down on the waiting table and went through the large mahogany doors into Senator Lincoln Chambers' office. In the middle of the room, two big, green, stuffy leather couches faced each other with a long, thin coffee table between. The senator was sitting at his desk, to the right, prominently framed by a large glass window with a perfect view of the Capitol Building. A man sat in the chair before the desk, someone Miles had never met but whom he recognized immediately—CIA Deputy Director Warren Thompson. The senator stood and came around to greet Miles.

"Miles, good to see you!" Senator Chambers, the senior senator from Illinois, was the sitting chair of the Senate Intelligence Committee. One of Miles' first campaign jobs was as an intern on Lincoln Chambers' run for Congress twenty-five years earlier, and he worked in the congressman's office on Capitol Hill that first term. Miles later worked on Lincoln's successful election and re-election runs for Senate. They'd been close ever since. They shook hands warmly.

"Thank you, Senator. I'm happy to see you as well. Thank you for setting up this meeting."

The senator motioned for the seated man to come over. "Miles, let me introduce you to CIA Deputy Director Warren Thompson."

"Nice to meet you, Sir." Miles fought down the urge to strangle the man.

"The pleasure is mine, Mr. Davis. I've heard a lot about you."

"I'm sure you have."

"Come, Gentlemen," the senator said. "Let's have a seat."

They sat on the sofa. A secretary came in through a side door with three glasses of water.

"You want anything else?" the senator asked.

The two men shook their heads.

"Thanks, Mary."

"My pleasure, Sir." She left the room.

"Miles, I briefed Deputy Director Thompson on what we discussed on the phone—the whole Yemen business and the agent you've been meeting. I believe what he has to say will be of great interest."

"Miles, first of all, I'm sorry to hear about all the troubles you've been through," Thompson said.

"With all due respect, Sir, I don't want your apology. You have an out-of-control agent threatening the life of an American citizen and..."

"Miles," the Deputy Director raised his hand. "Please let me speak. It's not what you think. We weren't involved in the attempted kidnapping of Sheikh Mohammed Abdullah or his assassination. We were as surprised as anyone by the piece in *Al Akhbar*. We didn't set up an operation in order to

93

blackmail you for access to your clients. Most important, we don't have an agent named John Carpenter."

Miles froze in shock, then he looked wide-eyed at the senator.

"It's true," the senator confirmed. "While you know we can't discuss classified information with those who don't have the required security clearance, I assure you that what the Deputy Director says is true. I felt it was important enough for you to hear it directly from him."

"So, who the hell have I been meeting with?" Miles asked.

"It appears John Carpenter is either an agent of another intelligence service, the Russians or the Chinese, or more likely he's a private contractor for an unknown benefactor who's trying to simultaneously smear the CIA and influence your clients, specifically Enrique Arenas in Colombia. The work we've already done seriously point toward a nongovernment entity."

"You mean a private company is behind this?"

"We aren't sure yet, Miles," the senator said. "Their emphatic interest in your work in Colombia and trying to convince Enrique not to nationalize Bancolombia if he becomes president speaks to someone or some organization with some serious financial interests in the country."

"You think the cartels are involved? Or FARC?" He felt like an ill-prepared student trying to navigate a pop quiz.

"We don't believe so," Deputy Director Thompson said. "The cartels don't have any money in legit banks, and FARC is too weak to care if the bank is nationalized."

"We could be looking at the tip of the iceberg of an international conspiracy here, Miles," the senator added. "We're hoping for your full cooperation, so we can get to the bottom of it."

"Yes, of course." Miles tried to reorganize the puzzle pieces in his mind.

The Deputy Director took out a recorder. "Can I record this conversation?"

The other two men nodded.

Miles told them in detail about his various interactions with John, from Yemen to the parks and restaurants in DC. As he related the story, he realized how ridiculous it sounded to assume the CIA was behind everything that had transpired.

Why didn't I realize this before? he wondered.

***

Two hours passed in what felt like a few minutes.

"Goddamn it, I feel like such an idiot," Miles said, as he finished his story. Running his hand through his hair, he drank the last of the water in his glass.

"Don't be so hard on yourself," the senator said. "Some of the greatest minds in history have been deceived, some worse than this. I'm happy, though, that you didn't let this John continue to harass you and had the confidence in me to help you in this situation."

"Yes, Miles," the Deputy Director said. "Thank you. Your story and description of this man will be invaluable for our task force. I'll be in touch if I need more information."

"Yeah. Sure." Miles felt as if he'd just run a marathon in thick mud.

All three men stood and shook hands. The Deputy Director let himself out and closed the door behind him.

Miles sat down and stared out the window at the Capitol Building. The setting sun laid a soft, orange glow on the building's white façade. A flock of Canadian geese flew in the background.

CHAPTER FOURTEEN

"Juanito, no running in the house!" Cecilia yelled, trying to hold her grip on her son, but he shook her off like a running back breaking from a tackle. She told him countless times not to run on the marble floors with his socks on, as he could slip and really hurt himself. But like any six-year-old boy in the world, discovering the lack of friction between socks and a slick floor was too exciting.

She stopped and watched him skid to the end of the hall, bounce off the wall, and dart down the adjoining corridor. Chapo, their Pomeranian, was hot on his heels, yapping and barking.

Sighing, she picked up his school backpack, shoes, and jacket from the floor and went into the kitchen. Mariela, the maid, was behind the island countertop busily preparing dinner. Water for pasta was just beginning to boil. The red sauce, already simmering on the stovetop, filled the air with a wonderful tomato, basil smell. Mariela was a wonderful cook, and Cecilia was grateful to have her in the household. She grabbed a raw carrot from the straining pot and put it in her mouth.

"Remember, Mariela," she said a little more patronizingly than she intended, "Dr. Enrique likes his carrots really soft. So does Juanito."

"Of course," Mariela said, hiding her rolling eyes from her boss.

Cecilia Galan threw her son's clothes into the mudroom leading to the back door and walked to where the wine was stored, browsed the bottles in the wine rack, and chose a 2005 Argentine Malbec. Popping the cork and pouring wine into a large, stemless wine glass, she moseyed into the living room, sat on the couch, turned on the TV, and swirled the deep burgundy red in her glass to let it breathe.

The evening news was about to start. She glanced at the mirror on the wall to her left, as the TV came on. She didn't admire or even recognize her stunning beauty. All she saw were the large, dark circles under her eyes, her uncombed black hair pulled back in a ponytail, and the ugly gray sports sweater she wore indoors that she'd had since college. She spent the entire morning giving interviews with newspapers, followed by a luncheon with a women's group. The afternoon was spent touring a local hospital full of wounded Colombian soldiers. Everywhere, a crowd of traditional media and paparazzi followed her every move. When she got home, she didn't even bother to shower. She just changed into her comfort clothes and pulled her hair back into a ponytail.

Taking her phone from her yoga pants' waistband, she began texting.

Cecilia: When will you be home, darling?

I'm getting old, she thought, frowning. Her husband's campaign was taking a serious physical and mental toll on her. He was never home, and they rarely saw each other. She'd been giving speeches and attending meetings with various interest groups around the country, rallying voter support for Enrique's campaign, for the past several weeks. They tried coordinating their travel schedules, but Alfredo and the *gringo* Miles said they'd cover more ground working separately.

"Divide and conquer," Miles said.

Easy for you to say, Señor Miles. You don't have a family.

97

She was a regular on morning talk shows and on the radio, though her appearances welled inside her a hellish convulsion of nerves and fear. Her natural beauty and easy smile belied the fact that she was incredibly shy and introverted.

"I need you to be the face of this campaign," Enrique pleaded when the campaign began, moments before he walked onstage to announce he was running.

She looked behind him and saw Alfredo, Miles, and David, huddled as always, whispering furiously to each other, and knew they were talking about her.

"I need you next to me up there." He made her look him in the eye.

"I can't, a*mor,*" she said with a sigh, wishing she were anywhere else. Her knees were ready to give out, and she shook visibly at the thought of standing on that large, open platform in front of the enormous crowd.

"Amor." He pulled her close and kissed her forehead. She wanted to stay in his arms forever, find a small piece of the world where they could take Juanito and their dog Chapo, and not have a care in the world. She felt safe only in Enrique's strong embrace. *Why was he doing this to me?* She thought.

"You'll be wonderful," he said. "Just take a deep breath and know you're standing beside me, the man who loves you and couldn't do this without you. We're running together. You'll be an incredible first lady for our country."

Love shone through his eyes, but she saw behind it his driving passion for becoming Colombia's next president. When he put his mind to something, he did it. He usually succeeded.

He would be a very good president, she thought.

She got up on stage that night, and the crowd went wild. Smiling, she stood beside her husband, as he gave a rousing speech and announced his candidacy. She kissed him when he finished, as instructed, and waved and smiled at their adoring fans.

The picture of their kiss was on the front page of all the newspapers and tabloids the following morning. Enrique and Cecilia were the new darlings of the media and the country.

She had to admit it was easier after that first night. She was a strong, proud woman, her father's daughter, something she was reminded of almost every day, but that didn't mean she didn't find it hard to do what she was told to do.

They were scheduled for an exclusive sit-down interview as a family with one of the country's leading journalists that weekend. She felt queasy about it.

The voice from the TV made her turn her head.

"...at about 15% and is now trailing businessman Enrique Arenas for the first time in this election," the anchorman said.

Great, she thought. *We might actually win.*

Her phone buzzed.

Enrique: Late my love. I'm sorry. Go ahead and have dinner without me.

"It appears that this bold new initiative of *Señor* Arenas to nationalize Bancolombia is really popular," the anchorman said.

Cecilia turned off the TV, feeling even sicker at the thought her husband might win. Ever since her father was assassinated, all Cecilia wanted was to hide from the world. She married a businessman because she was not only in love with him, but, almost as important, he wasn't a politician.

They don't assassinate businessmen, she thought. *They kidnap them sometimes, sure, but never kill.*

"*Señora,* dinner is almost ready," Mariela said, leaning her head around the corner. "Will Dr. Enrique be joining you?"

"Thanks, Mariela. Please get Juanito from his room. And no, Dr. Enrique will be home late and will eat later. Please prepare a plate for him and put it in the fridge."

"Will do, *Señora.*"

Cecilia gulped from her wine glass.

Cecilia: Ok. I miss u

Tears welled in her eyes. She wiped them away with her sweatshirt sleeve, hating herself for being so sensitive.

Enrique: I miss u too my love.

She put the phone down on the coffee table and sighed.

Be strong, Cecilia, she told herself. *Be strong.*

CHAPTER FIFTEEN

The phone rang several times before Bilal's voice answered.

"Hello, Miles," he said in Arabic. "It's good to hear your voice again. What can I do for you?"

"I don't want to discuss this over the phone," he replied in Arabic, glad to speak the language again. It always brought back fond memories of his time in Jordan with the young king. He was excited to have the opportunity to see him again in a few weeks. "I just wanted to let you know I'll be in Amman next month. I wanted to see if you could meet me there. I have important updates about the story that interests us both."

"I can make myself available."

"Just let me know where and when."

They said good-bye and hung up.

Miles stared across his mahogany desk, out the window toward the Capitol Building, pearly white against the background of the clear night sky. A few faint stars dotted the canvas behind it.

His mind jumped from thought to thought. He recalled the conversation in Senator Chambers' office, Khalid lying dead at the morgue, Lauren's silhouette getting smaller and smaller as she walked away, his upcoming trip to Amman, and what he would say to the king.

Of course, the Colombian election had started it all.

What the fuck's the matter with you, Miles? Get your

head on straight! Concentrate! he told himself.

Walking to the window, he rested his chin on his knuckles. *I need to tell the king I want the Saudis there when I arrive. It'll be important for me to tell them directly what I know.*

Should I loop David and Lisa into this? No. I don't want to stress them out more than they already are.

I need to follow the money, find out who stands to benefit if Enrique fails to nationalize Bancolombia. Always follow the money.

Lauren would probably be helpful. Should I call her? Text? Maybe an email would be OK? No. I should definitely call.

A knock on the door startled him from his trance. He turned to find Jason standing there.

"Hey, Boss. Sorry, I didn't know you were still here. I saw the light on and thought I'd turn it off."

"Hey, Jason. No worries. What are you doing here so late?"

"David asked me to compile the latest polling numbers and clips for Colombia. I was running regressions on the previous week's polling data and didn't get the new ones until this evening. They're ready now. I just sent them to him."

"Did you copy me, too?"

"Of course, Boss."

"Good."

"Do you need anything else before I leave?" Hoping the answer was no. He was exhausted and couldn't wait to climb into bed and get a few hours of sleep before doing the same thing for twelve hours again tomorrow.

"No. I'm good for tonight. Thanks, Jason."

"OK. See you tomorrow then." Jason took two steps and heard Miles call him back. With a soft sigh, he retraced his steps.

"Jason, do you know anything about shell corporations?"

Miles asked.

Confused, Jason said, "Yes, quite a bit, actually. I did a paper about them in college. What do you want to know?"

"I thought so. I'm not sure, really. How they operate, I guess? How easy are they to set up? How do they move money around? Things like that."

"Well," Jason mentally shuffled through his memory, like going through a filing cabinet to find the relevant information. "They are relatively easy to set up."

Miles went to the couch and motioned Jason to have a seat.

"You basically can do it online or over the phone with a lawyer who specializes in them. You come up with a name, pay a few hundred bucks, and, if you do it in Delaware, you can have it up and running the same day."

"Delaware? Why the fuck would anyone want to set up a shell company in Delaware?"

"Because they have some of the most-relaxed regulations and tightest secrecy and protection laws in the world. In fact, the U.S. is one of the top havens for shell companies in the world. You hear about Switzerland and the Caribbean island nations, but the U.S. is by far the biggest. Nevada and Montana are also good places. Even more, you don't have to attach your name to the entity you set up."

"Really?"

"Yeah. It's basically impossible for tax authorities or the law to identify the owner, because it's illegal to disclose that information."

"Hmmm. OK. What next, then? What do I do when I have a shell company?"

"Having a shell company in and of itself isn't illegal. Most of the Fortune 500 companies, if not all, have shells in various forms. It's what you can do with that entity that can get you into trouble. For example, you can open bank accounts using the shell company as the account holder, then transfer funds into those accounts. If you set up multiple accounts around the world, you can transfer funds through all those accounts, making the paper trail longer and harder to trace.

"You can even take it one step further and set up additional shell companies in other jurisdictions, like in Panama or Bermuda, which are whole subsidiaries of the shell company in Delaware, then have each of them open different bank accounts in places like Hong Kong or Switzerland, anywhere they have favorable banking laws, then pass the money through those."

"Wow. All of that is legal?"

"Well, not really. Doing that is money laundering. Where the issue arises, authorities are trying to get banks to pass laws over the information of who owns those accounts. Privacy laws in those jurisdictions are very tight, which makes it difficult to see who owns those companies, and, by default, who's controlling the money. The major banks have financial incentives to help those clients move the money around, because they can charge finance fees."

"So, how would one go about tracing money for a particular transaction, for example, or see how one might have invested in a certain bank in Colombia?"

Jason's eyes bulged, as he realized where Miles was going with his questions. Miles stared at him without moving a muscle.

"Ummm," Jason said, "you'd probably want to see who owns shares in the bank, then go from there, but you'd run into a wall eventually."

"What do you do when you hit a wall?"

"You'd have to know how to get through it or over it." Jason smiled at the mental image of Miles scaling a large wall. "You'd probably need someone on the inside who'd be willing to show you the information."

"Interesting." Miles stared at the pictures on the wall without seeing them. His mind raced, and he knew what he had to do.

Jason waited quietly, feeling awkward, until Miles remembered he was there.

"Thanks, Jason. Sorry for keeping you here. You can take off."

"Thanks, Boss. If want any more information, I'd be happy to help."

"I'll probably take you up on that, Jason. Good night."

"Good night, Boss."

CHAPTER SIXTEEN

David: You close?

Lisa: Yeah, traffic was bad. Pulling up to hotel now. 2 min.

Lisa: Did you pick up wine?

David: What do you think? ;)

Lisa: LOL just thought I would check! ;)

David set down his phone and smiled. He was in a hotel room on the third floor at the W Hotel in Washington, DC, overlooking the Treasury Department on 15th Street NW. The Washington Monument was visible on his left. The sun was almost below the horizon, highlighting the strands of clouds with an orange, pinkish hue. Traces of contrails crossed the sky like streaks of white and gray crayons. Stacy thought he was in New York for a meeting the next morning. Lisa told Stewart the same. Both promised to be back the following afternoon.

David opened the bottle of wine to let it breathe. Checking his teeth in the bathroom mirror, he gave a quick squirt of cologne on his neck and unbuttoned the second button on his shirt to expose a little more chest hair.

A light knock sounded on the door. David winked at himself in the mirror and walked to open it. "Who is it?"

"Room service," Lisa said from the other side.

"Sorry. I didn't order any room service."

"Oh, too bad. This order comes with a fantastic pair of tits."

David quickly opened the door. Lisa stood there in a tight black dress and a devilish smile.

"You're terrible."

"You love it."

"Mmm. Indeed."

He grabbed her by the waist and kissed her passionately. She threw her arms around his neck and returned the intensity. The heavy door swung closed by itself, as they moved toward the bed.

***

"Bishop takes pawn, D4." Lisa moved her white piece and removed David's pawn from the board.

"Interesting." David sat cross-legged, his back against the tall leather headboard. He was naked except for his boxers, and his hand gently stroked his chin. Lisa was completely naked, lying on her stomach on the opposite side of the board, content with her latest move.

"That, unfortunately for you, opens up this." He moved his queen across the board. "Checkmate."

"What? Shit!" She couldn't see how she'd missed that.

"You're getting much better, though."

Not wanting to accept defeat, she studied the board for an out. There wasn't one.

David got up and went to the table where the wine bottle stood. He brought it back to top off their glasses. He straddled her from behind and moved her red curls to one side, softly kissing her neck. She playfully recoiled and smiled.

"Seriously, you're getting much better," David said.

"I don't know. I do feel like you're actually playing against me now."

"My point exactly. I have to think now when I play you."

"And you didn't before?" She feigned and rolled him off her onto the bed. The chess pieces spilled from the board. Some rolled onto the floor. She got up and went to the bathroom.

David appreciated the view of her walking naked from behind. He reached to check his phone and scrolled through his notes until he found the poem he wrote a few days earlier. He scrolled Spotify and found the song he wanted—*In a Week,* by Hozier.

"I have another one to share with you," he said.

"Song?" she asked from the bathroom, flushing the toilet.

He set the phone down on the bed and sipped from his glass. "No, poem. You already know the song."

Lisa came out of the bathroom, lay on the bed, picked up his phone, and began reading.

Jump when I say jump, OK?
Two small hands clenched together,
Knees trembling,
A fragile bond of naïve trust
As the train rumbles down the track.
The sheer power of the moment,
More than either can control,
Or explain,
Or endure,
Yet never have either been so alive.
Does this scare you, Darling?
Do you trust me enough to do as I say?
To hold your heart in my hands
And be comfortable in the moment?
Empires have been lost for less, you know?
Peer over the edge, my love,
It's OK, I will hold you.
Look back to me if you need reassurance.

I'll do my best to time this jump,
Can you feel the heat of the engine train?
How far is the fall?
Is the water cold?
Will it hurt when we hit?
How cute of you to ask, my darling,
As if I've stood on this precipice before.
Breathe in this moment,
For countless hours have been spent,
And thousands of miles tread
Searching for this.
For what we just happened to stumble upon.
Here comes the train,
But hold on for just a little longer,
Trust me, I am as frightened as you are.
I just don't want this moment to end...
Jump when I say jump, OK?

"It does feel like we're standing on train tracks, doesn't it?" she asked.

"Yeah."

"Are you scared?"

He paused for a moment to think. "I don't know, Lish. I don't know if scared is the right word. I think it's more uncertainty than fear. I don't know what I want, and maybe I'm scared that what I want isn't in line with what I currently have. I don't want to deal with the consequences of that line of thought."

"How long have you and Stacy been married?"

"It'll be twelve years later this year."

"I can't believe you married so young."

"Yeah. My family and friends were surprised, too. I guess in hindsight I'm also surprised that I married so early. We were madly in love, and we just went for it. Now we have a family, a great house, two beautiful boys..."

"From the outside, you're the prototypical perfect family."

"Exactly, but it's an illusion. All I feel is suffocation. Don't get me wrong. I love my sons more than anything in the world, but there's something about my current status in life that makes me incredibly unhappy. I don't know why, Lish." Sipping from his glass, he saw it was almost empty. When he glanced at the bottle, there was only a little left.

"Do you still love Stacy?"

"I don't know."

"Then that's it."

"Yeah." He sighed. That was the first time he acknowledged the possibility that he didn't love Stacy anymore. The thought was simultaneously terrifying and exhilarating.

"Have you read *Eat, Pray, Love?*" she asked.

He gave her a weird look. "Of course not."

"Ha! Well, maybe you should. I think you'd find a lot in there that resonates. One line from the book has stuck with me. When she was writing about the decision to leave her husband, she said, 'The only thing more unthinkable than leaving was staying; the only thing more impossible than staying was leaving.'"

"Hmmm." The words hit him hard. Tears welled in his eyes, and he pretended to sneeze to hide them from Lisa.

She saw his glass was empty and reached for the bottle. After giving him the last of the wine, she kissed his forehead and petted his cheek. They looked at each other with unmistakable love.

She broke their gaze and carried the bottle to the desk near the window, placing it in the garbage can nearby. She heard the Hozier song restarting. David loved playing songs on repeat.

A fire truck siren whined nearby, and she heard the whirling blades of a helicopter overhead. *The typical sounds of DC,* she thought with a smile. *Along with David's music.*

She'd been in DC for four years, the longest she had ever stayed anywhere. Usually by that time, she had worn out her welcome, personally and professionally. She'd done it in New York, London, Paris, and home...

"I think Stacy knows," David said from the bed.

His statement shook Lisa from her melancholy reminiscence. "Why do you say that?"

"I can tell. She's been different since the birth."

"Maybe it's post–partum depression."

"She has that, too, but it's more than that this time."

"What will you do?"

"That's the question, isn't it? Anyway, I don't want to talk or think about it now. It's late, and I have only a limited time with you. I don't want to spend it talking about my wife. Come here."

She turned away from the window and faced him, leaning against the desk while she bit her lip. She lifted herself up onto the desk while arching her back and pushed out her chest. She flashed her coy smile, and David smiled back.

"Come over here," he said. "Now." Licking her lips, she moved slowly toward the bed.

David lowered himself on the bed and lay down. She climbed on top and straddled him, holding his arms down. He had a smug smile, as he looked up at her, her curls dangling in his face. She leaned down and kissed him, spreading open his mouth with her tongue. He gently held her bottom lip in his teeth. His hands moved down past her waist to rest on her ass. He grew hard again.

"Mmm," Lisa asked with a smile. "What's that?"

"A friend."

"Have I met this friend?"

"I believe you have."

"Looks like he wants to say hi again." She slid down, her breasts brushing against the length of his body. David's head rolled back in pleasure, as she removed his boxers with her teeth.

CHAPTER SEVENTEEN

John Carpenter walked down the dark corridor toward the end of the hall. The secretary behind the reception desk saw him approaching, clicked a button, and the yellow door behind her slid open. John entered the conference room and stood at the end of the long table, a bead of sweat running down his temple to his ear.

Three men in dark-black suits sat at the opposite end. The windowless room was too dark to see their faces, and the air was saturated with cigar smoke. The door slid closed behind him.

"It appears your position has been compromised," one of the shadows said.

"I didn't expect him to go directly to the Agency." Sweat formed in John's palms.

"An unfortunate turn of events, it seems," another one said.

"I'll take care of it."

"No need. We can take it from here."

From a corner behind John, a hulking man came up and slid a wire around his neck, pulling it tightly and crossing his hands behind John's head. John grabbed at the man's forearms, trying to slide his fingers under the wire. As he gasped for air, his knees gave, and he buckled to the floor.

The man squeezed tighter. John's face turned purple. His

hands desperately clutched at the table, but his sweaty palms couldn't get a grip.

A few moments later, John Carpenter fell lifeless to the ground, his eyes bulging, his tongue grotesquely protruding from his mouth. The man released his grip and put the wire into his pocket.

"You know what to do," said the first shadow who had spoken.

"Yes, Sir."

Two men came in and carried John's body out through a side door. The burly man followed them.

CHAPTER EIGHTEEEN

"Is it always fucking humid here?" Miles complained, wiping away the perspiration dotting his forehead. He took a cigarette from his shirt pocket and lit it with a yellow lighter. He allowed himself to smoke cigarettes only during the last week of a campaign. He loved the last week of campaigns.

"Sometimes Barranquilla isn't," Freddy said.

"Every time I come here, I sweat my balls off."

"This is probably the last time, at least for the work."

The election was only a few days away. Enrique had a comfortable lead in the polls, because the campaign was a smashing success. The controversial decision to nationalize Bancolombia ignited support for Enrique across the country. All the swing districts in the capital and the major cities were trending their way, and the other candidates floundered and bickered among themselves, not sure if they should attack Enrique's plan or embrace it. They had no idea what hit them. They were gasping for breath as he left them in the dust.

Even Miles had to admit it was the right call to win the campaign, though he still wasn't sure it was the right strategy for the country.

That's not why we were hired, remembering David's words. *Always remember that.*

Miles glanced at his watch and stubbed out his cigarette on the ground with his foot. His phone rang, and he saw it was an unknown number, so he clicked *Ignore* and put the phone away.

David emerged from the hotel with Lisa behind him. They came up to where Miles and Freddy stood and engaged in some nervous "Hellos" and "How was your night?" chitchat.

That day would be the last major speech of the campaign, what voters would most remember when they went to the polls. All the work the team had put in over the last few months would crystallize in the speech Enrique Arenas was about to give.

A convoy of four black cars awaited them. The lead car had four bodyguards, while the lag car was empty for the moment. Two bodyguards stood at the hotel entrance, with two others beside the last car. The two cars in the middle were for the passengers.

Enrique strode confidently through the hotel lobby and waved to the staff behind the counter. The guards opened the door, and Enrique approached the waiting group.

"What a great day for a campaign speech!" Enrique said. Though full of confidence, he still managed to convey a humble, personal charm. "It's great to see my *gringo* A-team again!"

It's charm that got him here, Miles thought. *He's a Ferrari racing against Hondas. We just know how to drive nice cars.*

"Good morning, Enrique," Miles said.

Enrique embraced each of them warmly. With his arms around David and Lisa, he smiled at the others. "I just wanted to say to you how happy I am that you came here to work. I know we had some difficult, tense moments, but I've been very impressed with what you've done. We wouldn't be here right now if it weren't for you."

"Come now, Enrique," Miles said. "It's you who will win this campaign. We just helped point you in the right direction."

"Say what you will, but I think we all know why we're here."

Everyone smiled, content with the work they'd done and glad the end was in sight.

"Enrique, we have to move," Freddy said. "The speech is scheduled to start in one hour."

"*Vámonos!*" Enrique shouted, clapping David and Lisa's backs. "David, ride with me. I want to review the notes of the speech on the way over."

"Of course, Enrique," David blushed and looked at Miles and Lisa.

"Lisa and Miles," Enrique continued, "you ride with Freddy in the other car."

"You're the boss," Miles said, surprised that Enrique asked David, not him, to ride together.

David wrote his last speech, Miles thought. *He's been point on most of the campaign issues from the beginning. He's gotten very close to Enrique in the last few weeks.* Pride and jealousy danced through Miles' heart. *My protégé. My son.*

David winked at Lisa and got in the car with Enrique. The others got into the trailing cars, and the convoy left.

The cars wound their way through the busy traffic. Enrique and David had dozens of loose papers on their laps. Enrique made final adjustments in red pen on his copy of the speech, and David looked through his own copy to make sure they had all the points included that scored well in recent focus groups.

"What about this part, David?"

David's Spanish had grown impressively better since the campaign began. He could write speeches directly in Spanish instead of English and then asking someone to translate them. He was proud of his accomplishment and joked with Enrique that he was even dreaming in Spanish.

"I think you should say here it's *with* the people I do this, not *for* the people. That's more inclusive."

"*Con la gente,* not *para la gente.* Good. I like that." Enrique made the change with his red pen.

In the car behind them, Miles' phone rang again. He checked caller ID, and once again, it was unknown. That time, he decided to answer.

"Hello?"

"Miles, thank… answered! It's…Thompson…ride in the convoy…"

The line went dead. A pit of worry grew in his stomach. He understood the name Thompson, and the voice was similar to CIA Deputy Director Warren Thompson. He stared at the phone, praying it would ring again.

It did.

"Yes? I'm here," Miles said. "Deputy Director Thompson, is that you?"

"Miles…credible intellig…attack…" The line died again.

"What's wrong?" Lisa became nervous at seeing Miles' reaction.

"I'm not sure, but I think we're in trouble."

Lisa's eyes bulged. "What kind of trouble?"

"Goddamn stupid fucking reception!" Miles snapped.

The driver and security guard looked back, then they followed Miles' incredulous gaze, as he stared at the car ahead of them.

The convoy came to rest at a stoplight. The sun beat down, and the temperature was almost at its high for the day. Peddlers hawked phone chargers, fruit, water, and maps. Small children wearing nothing more than dirty rags and torn T-shirts wove in and out of the cars, knocking on windows to beg for spare change. Two men approached the car Enrique and David were in from the left, their faces in ski masks. Both held AK-47 assault rifles.

"*Señor!*" the driver shouted.

Before the bodyguard in the passenger seat could draw his

gun, and just as Enrique and David looked up, the men unloaded a barrage of bullets into the car.

The security detail from the lead car jumped out and killed the assassins before they could return fire, but the damage was done. They approached with guns raised, shouting in Spanish, as guards from the rear of the convoy converged on the scene. The peddlers and homeless children screamed and scattered.

Drivers in the other cars ducked and covered their heads, while the bodyguards made sure the assassins were dead. Once that was confirmed, they secured the perimeter. One called for an ambulance and shouted into his phone for them to come as fast as possible. The cars nearest the convoy scattered.

The car holding Enrique and David was riddled with bullet holes. The driver and bodyguard were dead. Enrique and David both ducked to avoid the onslaught, but several bullets found David's ribs, arms, and legs. One pierced his kidney, and a few others penetrated his lungs. Enrique was hit, too, but only in the shoulder and right arm. Another bullet grazed his ankle, but no vital organs were hit. The way both of them fell and the angle of the approaching gunmen meant David's body became an unintentional shield for Enrique, absorbing most of the bullets. He lay unconscious on Enrique's lap, who was just recovering his senses.

"Oh, my God! David!" Lisa shouted from the car behind them. When she tried to open the door, Miles pulled her down.

"Stay here!" he shouted. "Stay down!"

"No, no, no!" she sobbed, unable to fully process what was happening.

They lay on the floor of the car until the security team gave the all-clear. Lisa jumped from the car, breaking free of Miles' grasp, and ran to the bullet-riddled car.

A security guard tried to stop her, but she shoved him

aside. "Get out of my way!" She didn't care if she would be shot.

She opened the door on David's side of the car and saw Enrique, now conscious.

"Help me get him out of the car onto the street," Enrique said. "We need to give him CPR. He's badly hurt."

"Are you OK, Enrique?" Lisa asked, helping take David's body from the car. When she looked down at him, all she saw was blood.

"I'm hit but I'll be fine. David's in bad shape."

The security detail ran up to move Enrique to a safe location, but he pushed them aside. "Give us space!" he shouted.

They reluctantly backed off and stood guard, scanning the growing crowd of onlookers for more assailants.

Miles ran over and helped Enrique and Lisa lay David down, then Miles began performing CPR. Lisa backed off and stood nearby in a daze, watching, as Freddy came up to the scene from the rear car.

"Oh, my God." Freddy ran to the other side of David's body and tore the sleeves off his shirt, tying them around David's wounds to try to slow the bleeding. In seconds, his hands were covered in blood.

When Miles blew into David's mouth, one of the bullet wounds that punctured his lung spat blood. Lisa almost fainted and turned her head away. Freddy covered the wound with his hand.

"Hang in there, David," Freddy said.

Miles alternated blowing into David's mouth and rhythmically pushing on his chest. One, two, three, four, five, blow. One, two, three, four five, blow.

Ambulance sirens became louder, as did the crowd around them. The security guards shouted, aiming their guns at the people, forcing them to stand back and let the ambulance through.

The paramedics intended to treat Enrique, because they'd been told the presidential candidate had been shot, but after he assured them all he had was a couple of flesh wounds, he ordered them to take David to the hospital immediately.

They secured David on a stretcher with an oxygen mask over his face and lifted him into the ambulance. A moment later, tires screeched, as they drove toward the hospital.

The spot where David lay was a puddle of dark-red blood. Another ambulance pulled up to take Enrique. Two of the convoy cars followed closely behind with Lisa, Miles, and Freddy inside.

Miles was covered in David's blood, and Freddy's shirt sleeves were torn off at the shoulder. Lisa closed her eyes, fervently wishing she was in a bad dream and silently cursing herself for not waking up already. Two bodyguards remained behind with the several police cars that arrived.

Miles stared at the floor of the car and muttered, "I'm gonna get those motherfuckers."

EPILOGUE

The clouds threatened rain, but Lisa knew they'd hold off for a while. They were a melancholy mirror for her mind. A crow landed on a branch in a nearby tree, squawking loudly.

My sentiments exactly.

She dug in her purse and found a cigarette pack. Taking one out and lighting it, she recalled a cigarette she had shared with David in a hotel room in Bogota one early morning. It felt simultaneously like yesterday and a lifetime ago, and it was still strong in her mind.

Was that the trip before, or the one before that?

She couldn't remember. It didn't matter. The memory was there nonetheless. David was in his boxers, sitting on the sill, the ashtray balanced on his knee. He had that intense, pensive look on his face that meant he was thinking deeply about something. That was also the expression he had when they made love, at least until he turned to face her and smile.

That smile...

David had been a smoker in college, and Lisa smoked only casually. "When the mood calls for it," David said.

It seemed appropriate to have one now, just like that morning in Bogota.

She dug into her purse to pull out a crumpled piece of paper. It was the last poem she received from David, the night before he was killed.

I search for the quiet peace that evades my mind,
Cluttered now with noise and fright,

Impossible, however, I seem to find,
Anything to remotely replace your light.
The Gauls are at the gate,
Our flank exposed, they show their might.
Revolutionaries demand our heads,
Off with them! They shout,
And put them on a spike!
Pyrrhus would surely smile,
For the losses have not been slight,
Destruction and debris all around our feet,
In order to reach this height.
So I will rage, and continue to rage,
Against the dying of this night,
A losing battle for sure,
Yet one I will fight.
Call me crazy, Dear,
I figured you might,
But on my board you are my queen,
And on yours I am the knight.

She smiled and thought of the time they lay naked in bed together, playing chess. "I was close to finally beating you, wasn't I?" she asked his tombstone.

Folding the piece of paper and replacing it in her purse, she took out a notebook. "I wrote one for you, too, last night."

Darkness, hold me,
Clutch me to your breast,
Tell me it's going to be fine,
I have nowhere else to go.
Your eyes, my windows to a world
I dared dream even existed,
Are gone now.
The secret hiding place is empty,
Yet the stories we told,
And the songs we wrote,
Will be forever there,

Abandoned,
But not forgotten.
Castaway,
Cast away to shores foreign, now mine.
Oh moonlight, pray for me,
Gently guide me into my tomorrows;
I am alone now,
And have nowhere else to go.

Tears pushed against her eyes, but she held them at bay. Her gaze lifted to stare out across the other tombstones. Only a few had flowers on them. Most looked abandoned and forgotten.

She heard footsteps behind her but didn't care enough to turn around.

"Hey, Kiddo," a familiar voice said.

Miles came up and put a hand on her shoulder. "Can I have one of those?"

He looked older.

David's death hit him just as hard, she realized.

She turned her gaze back to David's grave, thankful she hadn't begun crying yet. She handed Miles a cigarette and the lighter.

"What were you reading?" Miles asked.

"Oh, nothing, just some notes." She slid the notebook back into her purse and wiped her nose with the back of her hand.

"It's ironic that David's buried in a grave with a tombstone and everything," Miles mused, returning the lighter. "He always raged against cemeteries and how they were..."

"...a colossal waste of space," Lisa finished, a tiny smile on her lips.

She hadn't smiled since Colombia and that morning before the speech, where he promised they'd be together later that evening.

"Yeah," was all Miles could muster. "How are you holding up?"

"As well as I can, I think. I saw the results come in yesterday. Looks like Enrique won comfortably."

"Yeah."

After Enrique survived the assassination attempt, his popularity soared even higher. He won the election handily.

They stood in silence for a few minutes, comforted by each other's presence and the shared grief for someone they both loved. It hadn't mattered that David wasn't Miles' son, or that he wasn't Lisa's husband. Life conspired against their will to thrust them together. The experiences they shared solidified the bond each had with David until it became unbreakable even at his death.

Subjects to circumstance, David wrote in one of his poems. That line stuck in her mind like a cut in her mouth that she couldn't stop feeling with her tongue. Chance circumstance made them collide, like two asteroids meeting in the deep void of space. *That's what he meant,* she thought.

She thought of it differently, however. She believed everything happened for a reason, and that their two souls were meant for each other. Fate would always bring them into each other's orbits. She stayed up at night since returning from Bogota, crying in her bedroom, looking up at the moon and stars to see if they had any clues or ideas that would explain the reason behind this tragedy. Because if everything happened for a reason, then David's death was supposed to happen like it did, just like everything that preceded it was preordained.

She couldn't understand why it happened. It went against everything they planned, everything that led them to be where they finally were. David had already begun divorce proceedings with Stacy, and Lisa had broken off her engagement with Stewart. They planned to wait a couple months before making it official, even though they knew people would be suspicious of the timing.

They didn't care. They found each other, no matter that it took several years, an affair, a broken engagement, and the destruction of a marriage before it happened. They were in love.

"I'm going to take some time off for myself, Miles."

"I figured you would. Take as much time as you need. Come back when you want."

The crow on the branch gave another long squawk. A cold wind ruffled the ends of Lisa's skirt. Miles opened his umbrella, as rain began to fall. Lisa began crying, then sobbing, as she buried her head against Miles' chest.

View other Black Rose Writing titles at www.blackrosewriting.com/books and use promo code **PRINT** to receive a **20% discount** when purchasing.

BLACK☘ROSE
writing™